BEHIND THE RANGES

other books
by Stephen W. Meader

THE BLACK BUCCANEER

DOWN THE BIG RIVER

LONGSHANKS

RED HORSE HILL

AWAY TO SEA

KING OF THE HILLS

LUMBERJACK

THE WILL TO WIN AND OTHER STORIES

WHO RIDES IN THE DARK?

T-MODEL TOMMY

BAT

BOY WITH A PACK

CLEAR FOR ACTION

BLUEBERRY MOUNTAIN

SHADOW IN THE PINES

THE SEA SNAKE

THE LONG TRAINS ROLL

SKIPPY'S FAMILY

JONATHAN GOES WEST

HE STOOPED QUICKLY, PICKED THE BOY UP LIKE A SACK OF
MEAL, AND FLUNG HIM OVER HIS RIGHT SHOULDER

Behind the
RANGES

by *STEPHEN W MEADER*

ILLUSTRATED BY EDWARD SHENTON

SOUTHERN SKIES

ISBN 978- 1-931177-50-4 cloth
ISBN 978-1-931177-51-1 paperback

SOUTHERN SKIES

LITTLE ROCK, ARKANSAS
www.southernskies.com

Dedication

*The republication of this book is dedicated to Alan Box---
business genius, bon vivant, world's greatest partner---by his
friend of forty years, Jerry Atchley.*

ACKNOWLEDGMENTS

To Irving Clark, in whose home on Hunt's Point I first heard the story of the Olympics; to Herb and Lois Crisler, who know the wilderness mountains from long and intimate experience; and to Ernest and Richard Walter, who have contributed their time and enthusiasm to this book—my deepest gratitude.

S. W. M.

LIST OF ILLUSTRATIONS

BEHIND THE RANGES

One

THE BIG AIRLINER BEGAN TO LOSE SPEED
and altitude. Dick Randolph leaned closer to the window, peering out through the flying wisps of fog. He
could sense a slower beat in the rhythm of the four huge
engines as the throttles were cut back.

"Dad," he exclaimed, "those clouds are breaking away!
Just for a second I thought— Hey, look! There it is
again!"

Off to the southeast, where he pointed, something white and vast appeared for a moment, vanished, then came into view once more.

"That's it, all right," said his father. "Your first sight of Mount Rainier! Sort of takes your breath away, doesn't it?"

Dick's mouth was open, his eyes staring. "Gee!" he murmured. "I didn't know anything could be so darn big. And it's forty miles away!"

"Just about that," Dr. Randolph nodded. "We're over Tacoma now. See the shipyard down there? And the lumber mills up along the shore to the west? That's Puget Sound—and the big wooded island across the water is Vashon. We'll be landing in a few minutes now."

The lighted panel on the forward bulkhead flashed the words "No Smoking. Fasten seat belts."

Dick fumbled for the strap and buckle and pulled the belt tight. He had made landings before in the 3000-mile trip across the continent, but this time he felt an added thrill of excitement. This was journey's end. He had reached the country of his dreams—the Pacific Northwest!

The plane circled, well below cloud level now, and dropped steadily earthward as it swung into the wind for its final approach to the runway at Boeing Field.

"Coming into Seattle," announced a smiling stewardess. "Keep your seat belts fastened, please, and remain seated after we land."

The plane skimmed the runway, the huge tires touched with a barely perceptible bump, and in a minute or two they were taxiing easily up in front of the terminal. When Dick and his father came down the ramp they stepped out into bright sunshine.

Dr. Randolph drew a deep breath. "There's nothing like a clear summer morning in this Puget Sound country," he said. "Feel that northwest wind! Cool and bracing! Too bad there's a haze over the Olympics. They're off there to the northwest. Don't hit you like the first glimpse of Rainier, but they're quite a sight all the same."

The luggage was brought from the plane and the Randolphs claimed their bags, which were put aboard the airline limousine. Dick carried his precious camera, as he had done all the way west. He didn't want anything to happen to that. To a great extent the success of the trip would depend on the pictures he hoped to get.

It had been back in May—nearly two months before—that the plan had begun to take shape. His father, one of the nation's foremost botanists, had been commissioned by the Smithsonian Institution to collect and classify some little-known species of heather and other flora found only in the high Alpine meadows of the Olympic Mountains. To Dick, seventeen and just finishing his last year in high school, the expedition sounded dull enough. At the moment he was more interested in the track team, Commencement and the prospects of a summer job. He planned to enter college in the fall, and wanted to earn a little money to help pay his way. The salaries of even the most noted botanical authorities are likely to be modest, and Dick knew that his father's was no exception.

Then one evening he came home to their comfortable little house in Alexandria and found Dr. Randolph bent over a map on the living-room table.

The botanist looked up, beaming through his spectacles. "Believe I'll get quite a thrill out of this trip," he said. "I wish there was some way to take you with me, son."

Dick laughed. "Sure, I'd give a lot to see the Coast," he replied. "But collecting heather doesn't sound too exciting."

"Take a look at this map," said his father mildiy. "Here's the Olympic Peninsula. It's bigger than the state of Connecticut. And it's the wildest section left in the United States. Wilder, probably, than the country Daniel Boone hunted over. Bigger trees, bigger mountains, and about as many animals."

"Honestly?" said Dick. "What kind of animals?"

"Oh, bear, cougar, elk, deer and a few mountain goats up on the high ridges. There are no roads into the interior. I'll have to go in afoot, with a back-pack, and most of my work will be up around seven thousand feet— above timber line. Not that I won't see a lot of timber," he added. "The finest virgin forests left in America are right there on the Peninsula."

The boy's eyes had begun to shine. "That *would* be

something to see," he murmured. "The big game, too—cougar and elk! And the mountain-climbing and camping! Gee, if I didn't have to get a job this summer, I'd sure like to be along."

His father leaned back and looked at him thoughtfully. "You know," he said, "there might be some way—hmm—I think I'll speak to the director of the Natural History Building. It would be a big help if I had a husky young woodsman with me. Let's see what I can do."

That was the way things stood for the next two days. The more Dick thought about the trip, the more excited he grew. He went to the high school library and read everything he could find about the Olympic National Park. To his amazement he discovered that there were large parts of the peninsula about which nothing seemed to be known. The maps showed unnamed peaks, and sections many square miles in area were marked "unexplored."

On the second evening his father had news for him. "If you can go to see Dr. Castleman tomorrow after school," he said, "he may have something to tell you. And one thing I wish you'd do. Take along some of your best photographic work—especially those color films."

The interview with the Smithsonian's Natural History director was surprisingly successful. Dr. Castleman knew good camera work when he saw it and his comments on Dick's pictures gave the boy courage to speak up.

"Doctor," he began, hesitating a little at his own

brashness, "I guess you know I'd like to go with my father on his trip west. Well—I've been studying up on Pacific Coast fauna. I've always been interested in animals—out at the Zoo and here in the Natural History Building. Those habitat groups of yours, with the painted backgrounds, are really swell."

Dr. Castleman was looking at him quizzically. "Yes?" he said. "Go on."

Dick flushed and stammered. "Well, I—I don't want to sound critical—but there's one kind of animal you haven't got. The Zoo hasn't it either, but there's a reason for that. It probably can't live at low altitudes."

The director's eyebrows went up. "This missing species," he remarked with a twinkle. "It wouldn't be the silver marmot by any chance?"

"Why, yes," said Dick, surprised. "That's what I meant."

Dr. Castleman nodded. "Very interesting little animal," he replied. "Rare on this continent, too. About the only place they're found in numbers is in those high rocks of the Olympics. I agree a good specimen would help our collection. Now go on with your idea."

The boy leaned forward earnestly. "I'd like to try to get a couple of silver marmots for a habitat group," he said. "And at the same time I could take color films of the places where they live—so that the setting for the group would be just right."

"That's odd," smiled the director. "I was about to

make you the same proposition myself. I think you've got the job, young man."

.   .   .

Dick was thinking of those parting words now, as he clutched his small reflex-type camera in its leather case and stared out the limousine window. They whisked past the huge Boeing plant, catching a glimpse of new airplanes parked on the apron.

"Hey!" the boy exclaimed, craning his neck in an effort to look back. "That big double-decked one was a Stratocruiser, I'll bet!"

As he might have expected, his father's eyes were on something else.

"Sorry," said the botanist, "I was looking at the lawn in front of the office, there. Nice turf—probably bluegrass—*Poa pratensis.*"

Dick shook his head and said no more. He had long since discovered that scientists were strange people.

The tall buildings of a big and busy city loomed up ahead. In a few minutes the limousine passed the twin railroad stations and whirled up Fifth Avenue. After a stop at the Olympic Hotel to discharge passengers, it went on to the New Washington, where Dick and his father had made reservations.

Their room, the boy was glad to find, was on the west side, and high enough to command a fine view of Seattle's famous harbor. Ships from all the world lined the docks below, and two gray cruisers and a carrier were anchored farther out. Tugs and ferries bustled back and forth in the wide roadstead, their hoarse hooting rising cheerfully above the hum of street traffic.

"All right, son," said Dr. Randolph, "you go ahead and explore the town if you like. I've got some telephoning to do, and I may go over to the Forest Service headquarters. You can meet me here at the hotel for lunch."

Nothing could have pleased Dick better. He left the lobby, crossed Second Avenue and started down Stewart toward the waterfront. One thing he had already noticed about Seattle was its hills. To his eyes, used to the level thoroughfares of the national capital, these crosstown streets seemed to climb and descend at dizzy angles —steep as the roof of a house. Cars went up them in low gear, and when people parked, they always cramped their wheels against the curb.

The boy walked south on First Avenue, fascinated by the Alaska outfitters' stores, where fur-lined parkas and mukluks were displayed side by side with plaid lumberjack shirts and high-laced work boots. He descended to Alaskan Way—the broad, truck-crowded street that ran along the docks. There were pleasant smells in the cool wind that blew off the Sound. Fish and salt water and fresh-cut fir lumber. Weatherbeaten seamen, in from the Pacific, rubbed elbows with smooth-cheeked young Navy men on shore leave.

Dick paused at a dingy old curio shop, staring at the

totem poles, whales' teeth, walrus tusks and Indian mats, woven from cedar bark. He bought a picture post card to mail home to his mother, then wandered on along the waterfront.

It was nearing noon when he turned eastward past the Smith Tower and made his way back uptown through the department store district. His father was waiting for him in the hotel lobby.

"Everything is moving splendidly," Dr. Randolph announced, as they ordered their lunch. "We can start tomorrow. The letter from the Secretary of the Interior smoothed the way for us, and we'll have the help of the Forest Service right from the start. You'll be allowed to take traps into the National Park and bring out any silver marmots you can catch."

"That's great," Dick beamed. "How do we get across to the Olympics? Are you going to hire a car?"

"No, indeed. That's all taken care of. We'll go over in a Forest Service car and they'll assign a ranger to guide us all the way up to our camping place. I tell you, these people out here are wonderful!"

Dick described his sightseeing tour while they ate Dungeness crab and fresh salmon steak. "I'd like to get a look at Lake Washington before we leave here," he said. "Do you suppose there's a bus that'll take me over there?"

"Better than that," Dr. Randolph chuckled. "As it happens, I'm going over to Hunt's Point, across the lake, this afternoon. One of the National Park commissioners lives over there, and a man from the Forest Service is taking me in his car. I'm sure he'll be glad to have you go along."

The Forest Service official turned out to be a big, quiet-spoken man of middle age, named Joe Evans. An ex-ranger, he was familiar with all the wilderness country of the Northwest. He pointed out some of the city's landmarks as they drove along the hilly streets overlooking Lake Washington. Then they swooped down to cross the famous floating concrete bridge. To Dick it seemed as solid as dry land, even though a brisk wind was whipping the lake to whitecaps on each side of the four-lane highway.

On the other shore they entered a wholly different kind of country. Winding roads led through green woodland and past little suburban settlements. On Hunt's Point itself the car rolled along in the shadow of giant fir trees that must have stood there unmolested for centuries. Occasionally they could glimpse gracious houses, set back from the road on either hand. At the entrance to one of these their driver turned in.

Mr. Carter, the commissioner, was there to welcome them. He led the way around the big, sprawling frame house to a terrace that faced the lake. There were comfortable chairs there, and the three older men sat down to talk while Dick looked about him in wonder.

Never had he seen such a fairyland. Around him were immense firs, three or four feet through at the butt and towering more than a hundred and fifty feet into the air. The breeze sighed through their branches and stirred the fronds of the huge green ferns that clustered about their feet. Down a flagstoned path was the blue lake, with a swimming dock, a rack of canoes and a trim, white sailboat rocking at its mooring. And off to the east, lifting above the woods on the opposite shore, were the distant ranges of the Cascades.

He went down to the dock, trying to imagine what it would be like to live in such a place—close to a big city, yet surrounded by so much natural, unspoiled beauty. A youngster like himself, he decided, could have a lot of fun out here, with all the sailing, fishing, hunting and exploring any boy could desire, right at his back door.

He felt at home in this country, yet nothing was quite the same as on the eastern seaboard where he had grown up. The grass and foliage were greener, the trees bigger. Even the flowers and birds were strange to him.

There was a tree on the bank above the water. Its leaves were big and glossy like those of a magnolia, and where the sun fell on its smooth trunk the bark took on a ruddy orange hue, warm and bright as flame. It was a madrona tree—he knew because he had heard his father use the name that morning—and it seemed to him a kind of symbol of the difference between East and West, Atlantic and Pacific. The United States, he told himself, certainly covered a lot of territory.

"Come on, Dick," Dr. Randolph called from the terrace. "We've got to get our outfits in shape for a start tomorrow."

Evans drove them back to town and went up with them to their hotel room, where he checked over the clothing and equipment they had brought.

He approved the heavy flannel shirts, hobnailed mountain boots, wool socks, tough khaki trousers and shorts.

"We used to wear heavy jeans we called 'tin pants,'." he said, "but you won't be fighting thick brush, so you probably won't need 'em. Those eiderdown sleeping-bags you've got are just right—warm, light and waterproof. And your cooking kits are good. Let's see—camp ax, hunting knife, matches. We'll buy food supplies at Port Ludlow tomorrow. Looks like you're all set. I'll be here with the car at eight tomorrow morning if you can be ready then."

They thanked him and agreed to the time he set. When he had gone, Dr. Randolph went to the window and looked out to the west.

"There they are, son," he said softly.

Dick stepped forward, and as he looked his breath came quicker. In the sunset light the snowy peaks of the Olympics stood sharp and clear. Range after saw-toothed range they stretched away, seemingly to infinity. The boy's jaw set. Tomorrow he would set out to meet their challenge.

Two

THE RANDOLPHS ATE AN EARLY BREAK-
fast, left the suitcases containing their city clothes with
the hotel porter to keep, and checked out of their room.
At the stroke of eight they were waiting outside, with
their duffel piled on the sidewalk.

It was a blowy, bright morning, with high clouds sailing over from the southeast.

"Two fair days in succession," Dr. Randolph commented. "That's pretty good for Seattle. Still, I've never been here before in July, so maybe it's normal for this time of year."

Joe Evans' sedan pulled in at the curb and in a moment he was helping them stow their equipment in the rear trunk.

"We're getting away in good time," he said. "Ought to make the nine o'clock ferry at Edmonds with a few minutes to spare."

They drove northward through the early morning traffic, crossed the high bridge over the Lake Washington Canal, and headed out of the city on U.S. 99. Within half an hour they were coming down to the ferry landing at Edmonds.

The tide was out. As the car made its way along the pier they could see acres of mudflats below them, and the tall piles stood up nakedly, the lower portion of each one crusted with barnacles.

A score of cars and trucks were already aboard the boat. Evans drove down the sloping gangplank, parked in line, shut off the engine and set the handbrake. "This ferry we're on is the *Klickitat,*" he said. "She's one of the bigger boats. We've got a long ride, so we might as well go up on deck where we can see the sights."

With a long hoot of the whistle the ferry pulled out from shore and headed north. Across the Sound the peaks of the Olympics came into view, cold and aloof against the high clouds.

"That's where you're going, folks," said Evans. "Right up there on top. See those twin peaks to the southwest? They're called the Brothers. The big one right across from us is Mt. Constance. Don't believe we can see Olympus. It's 'way over behind that ridge of white peaks."

Dick had a hard time dragging his eyes away from the mountains, but there were other things to see. Forty or fifty people were clustered on the forward deck, talking, laughing and enjoying the clear sunshine. Most of them were countrymen or woodsmen from the peninsula. The boy saw several buxom farm women carrying big string bags loaded with purchases. There were bearded lumberjacks in calked boots and a few sleepy-looking Indians slouching by the rail.

The breeze freshened and whitecaps dotted the blue water. A rusty freighter, inbound from the Strait of San Juan, came slogging past, and a tug puffed southward with a half-mile string of timber rafts in tow.

Joe Evans pointed to the northeast. "That green shore up there," he said, "is Whidbey Island. There's about forty miles of it—reaches all the way to Deception Pass. The big, flat-topped mountain you see over Whidbey is Mt. Baker."

The ferryboat held its course northwestward for nearly an hour, passed the wooded shore of Point No Point, then swung to the west, skirting Foul Weather Bluff. Dick looked eagerly ahead. The snow-capped mountains loomed ever nearer, and somewhere below them, at the foot of those forested slopes, was Port Ludlow.

"It's funny," said the boy after a while. "I've been looking for a long time, and I can't see any town."

"We're heading straight for it," Evans grinned. "How far off do you reckon that shore line is?"

"It looks like about a mile," Dick estimated.

"You're judging by the size of the trees," said the ex-ranger. "That's what throws most Easterners off. Those Douglas firs are more'n twice as tall as what you're used to. I'd guess we've got nearly three miles to go yet."

As it turned out he was right. A full five minutes later the boy made out a white painted water tower, the stack of a sawmill and a gray patch that might be the weathered side of a frame building. At last, when the trees on the shore seemed to be only a stone's throw away, he saw a tiny speck moving on the rocky beach below them. It was a man, no bigger than an ant in contrast to the towering firs.

The ferryboat slowed down and drifted in toward the dock. Down on the mudflats an old Indian in a ragged blanket coat was walking slowly, half crouched on his bow legs, holding a long-handled shovel in front of him. As Dick watched, the Indian made a sudden lunge, driving his implement deep into the mud. He dug feverishly for a moment or two, then gave it up and moved on with a grunt of disgust.

"Digging for geoducks," Evans chuckled. He pronounced it "gooyducks" like all good Puget Sound folk.

"They're clams pretty near as big over as a football," he explained. "The necks on 'em are two or three feet long and thicker'n a piece of garden hose. Hard to catch, though. They'll pull their necks down and settle into the muck mighty fast if they feel the vibration of a footstep anywhere close to 'em."

"How can you tell where they are?" Dick asked. "Do the necks stick up out of the mud?"

"No," said the Forest Service man. "The end of the neck is just at the surface and hard to see. But as you walk along you'll see a stream of water squirt up, five or six feet high. Gets you right in the eye, sometimes. That jet of water comes out of Mr. Gooyduck's neck, when he yanks it in."

The boy would have liked to wait and see one of the strange creatures captured but it was time to get back in the car. Starters whirred, engines chugged into action, and the line of vehicles climbed the steep gangway to the dock. Soon they were in the town itself and Joe Evans was parking the sedan in front of a sprawling frame store building.

Dick had seen general stores in other country towns back East. But he had never been in one quite like this. After the bright morning sun outdoors, it seemed very dark inside at first. Then he made out the worn counters, piled with overalls and work shirts, rubber boots and felt hats, bolts and nails and shotgun shells, cracker cartons and pickle jars. Behind them rose dusty shelves of other merchandise—shoes and piece goods, canned beans and tomatoes and peaches. The floor was cluttered with still more things, ranging from flour barrels to work harness, but in the middle of the store was one cleared space, surrounding a tall black stove. Here three or four assorted characters slouched in rickety chairs, chewing tobacco and whittling.

One of these figures—the only one without a hat on—got creakily out of his chair at their entrance. He was a stocky, gray-haired man of middle age.

"Hiya, Jed," Joe Evans greeted him. "Got a couple of *chechakos* here that need to be outfitted. How's your supply of self-rising flour? They'll need bacon, tea, sugar, salt and waterproof matches, too."

Twenty minutes later the packages of supplies were wrapped and paid for. Dick, meanwhile, had been rummaging among the merchandise piled on the floor.

"Look here, Dad," he said. "Here's one thing I ought to have—a number-two jump trap. Think that'll hold a marmot, Mr. Evans?"

The ex-ranger picked up the trap and tested its spring. "Well," he said, "it's strong enough, I'd say. Don't know whether you'll ever get one to step in it, but if he did it ought to hold him."

They bought the trap, took their other bundles and returned to the car. The road out of the little town passed through a foothill country of farms, second growth and cut-over land, where young firs were shooting up amid the stumps and brush. After a few miles they swung southward, heading for Quilcene and U.S. Route 101, the main Olympic highway.

Dick sat in front beside the Forest Service man, and he spent most of that ride leaning forward, drinking in thrill after scenic thrill. The mountains were so close now that he had to look up almost vertically to see their misty summits. The road wound through narrow valleys where the dense growth of giant firs turned the forenoon into twilight. Occasionally he caught a glimpse of weathered farm buildings and cattle grazing on green bottom lands at the foot of the crags, but for the most part they drove through forests and more forests.

At Quilcene there was a glimpse of blue water—an arm of the Hood Canal called Dabob Bay, the ex-ranger told them. Then they were on the hard-surfaced highway and moving south again. Just to the west of Mt. Walker they entered the National Forest for the first time, though Dick could notice no difference in the rugged, wooded landscape.

They stayed on the main road and skirted the placid waters of the estuary for several miles.

"Here's where I show you some real Olympic driving," said Evans, as he swung the car into a narrow black road that led up through the woods to the right.

"This is the Dosewallips trail," the forester explained. "The Dosewallips River runs down there in the valley. You could hear it if the car wasn't making so much noise.

Our main Ranger Camp is a dozen miles or so up the river, and that's where you'll stay tonight."

It was a wild ride, even at the speed of fifteen to twenty miles an hour that Evans maintained. The trail climbed over ledges and swooped down into gulleys. Only wide enough for one car, it had been hacked out of the rough mountainside in many places. The tires bumped over roots, and bushes scraped the top and sides of the sedan. Once, as they came over a rise, Dick caught a momentary view that made him hold his breath. Above the huge black V of the canyon ahead stood a rocky peak, snow-crested and gigantic.

"Camp's right up there at the foot of that mountain, around the bend," said Evans.

Ten minutes later they went up a twist of the trail, pitched over the top and pulled up before a wide-eaved log cabin. The Ranger Camp stood in a tiny clearing, backed by the mountainside and flanked by a pair of Douglas firs that were nearly ten feet through at the butt. In front of it, just beyond the trail, the wooded ground dropped away abruptly to the river bed, hundreds of feet below.

A tall, lean woodsman in well-worn khaki came out of the cabin and approached the car.

"Howdy, Alec," Evans greeted him. "These are the folks from the East I 'phoned you about. Dr. Randolph—Dick—meet Alec Campbell, our Chief Ranger."

They shook hands and Campbell gave them a hand

with the unloading.

"We've got the trip all set up for you," he told them cordially. "One of our men's starting north tomorrow and he can guide you right up to Four Lakes Basin. It's only half a day out of his way. Meanwhile there are cots here for you tonight—about the last soft beds you'll sleep in till you come back, I reckon."

Inside the cabin they found themselves in a big, comfortable room with a work table and telephones at one end, a stone fireplace and easy chairs at the other, and a series of detailed Forest Service maps pinned up on the walls. At the back were several small sleeping rooms and a kitchen presided over by a wrinkled Chinese who beamed with pleasure when he learned there would be guests for dinner.

As the meal was being put on the table a tanned young man in ranger's clothes came in the door. He slipped a big pack off his shoulders and set it in a corner before coming forward to be introduced.

Dick liked him from the moment he gripped his hard, brown hand. His name was Dan Craig, and he was the ranger detailed to be their guide.

"Dan's been with us a year," Campbell told the Randolphs when Craig had gone to wash up. "Studied forestry before he went into the Army. And incidentally he was an All-Coast tackle at the University of Washington. He had a first-class war record and came out as a sergeant. All in all, he's a pretty able young fellow."

The food prepared by Fong Yee was delicious. There were steaks and baked potatoes, tender string beans, a salad of tomatoes and lettuce, and fluffy hot biscuits.

Dr. Randolph commented on the excellence of the fare and Campbell nodded. "We have to set a good table here," he said. "When the boys come in from a two weeks' patrol, they're starved for the kind of grub that can't be carried in a pack. You'll be pretty hungry yourselves by the time you get back here."

When the meal was over, Dan Craig unfolded a large-scale map and showed them their route.

"We'll make an early start tomorrow," he told them, "and get up to the head of the Dosewallips by night. There's a lean-to shack there where we can sleep. The next day we'll climb this ridge and move north. If we make twelve miles we'll be doing well. That'll put us right up under the peaks, and with luck you'll be over the rim into Four Lakes Basin while it's still daylight."

He hesitated, looking around at Dr. Randolph. "There's just one thing," he said, with some embarrassment. "This is tough country—maybe the toughest in the world. If you've never done any mountain climbing with a heavy pack—well, you see what I mean?"

The little scientist smiled at him. "I don't blame you for wondering," he replied. "But I'm really stronger than I look. Wiry is the word, I believe. Dick is the athlete of the family but I'll do my best to keep up with him."

"Okay," the young ranger laughed. "I can carry a few

extra pounds so we'll keep your packs as light as possible. We use a special kind of pack-board up here. It's called a 'Trapper Nelson.' Ever wear one?"

He went to a store-closet and brought out a pack frame. It consisted of a pair of straight pieces of wood, held together by three curved wooden braces. Around it was stretched a width of canvas, laced tight down the middle. The vertical sticks extended about six inches beyond the covering at the top and two inches at the bottom. Broad webbed shoulder straps passed through slits in the canvas and were attached to the cross braces. And sewed on to each strap was a soft sheepskin pad to ease the load on the shoulders.

"These things are light and strong," said Craig. "Cool, too, because there's air space between your back and the load. You can hang extra stuff on those wooden horns at the top if you like. The knapsack fastens to these rings in the sides so it can't swing or slip. Here—try this one on for size."

The pack frame turned out to be a little too big for Dr. Randolph but fitted Dick almost perfectly. A smaller one was brought out for the botanist, and the ranger helped them stow their supplies in the roomy knapsacks. By the time the rolled sleeping-bags were buckled under the top flaps, each pack weighed close to fifty pounds. In addition, Dick would be carrying his camera in its case, strapped to his belt, and the hunting knife in a sheath. He began to understand why Craig had been doubtful about their ability to go through with the trip.

Dusk came early in the mountain valley. By five o clock, when the boy went outside for a look at the camp, the sun was behind the high peaks to the west, and the air had a chill in it.

He shuffled through the smooth carpet of brown needles that covered the ground. Above him, the two enormous firs reached upward into the gloom, their vast trunks bare of limbs for a clear hundred feet. At the foot of one of them he saw a figure kneeling. It was his father, busily examining a small plant that grew among the roots.

Dick smiled and crossed the road to the edge of the canyon. The dark tops of firs and hemlocks stretched away below him, and he could hear the musical murmur of flowing water, far down in the valley bottom.

He felt a tingling in his veins. "This is it," he thought. "This is the jumping-off place. From here on it's us against the wilderness."

He turned to go back to the cabin, and saw the Chief Ranger strolling toward him.

"Nice, quiet evening," Campbell remarked. "Looks like good weather for your start."

At that moment an unearthly scream came echoing down from the upper valley, and Dick almost jumped out of his skin.

"Cougar," said Campbell with a yawn. "Lots of 'em around. Sometimes you hear 'em yelling all night."

Three

WITH THE DARKNESS CAME A MOUNTAIN
chill that made the wood fire in the cabin welcome. Evans
had driven back to Seattle, but Campbell and Craig
joined Dick and his father before the blazing logs.

The Chief Ranger lighted a brown corncob pipe and
puffed at it contentedly.

"Hearing that cougar holler," he said, "made me think
of the movie magnate that came up here a while back.

He went out for a walk one night and heard a cat yell like that. Ran all the way back to camp and wouldn't stir out for two days."

"Aren't cougars pretty dangerous?" Dick asked.

"Shucks, no," Campbell grinned. "Never heard of one attacking a human in the thirty years I've been up here. Of course, they're mean customers when they're cornered or wounded. There was an Indian hunter over on the Elwha River that got mauled pretty bad a couple of years ago, but it was his own fault. Had a big cougar treed and his aim was so bad he hit the limb and just grazed the cat. Cougar landed plumb on top of him. If he hadn't had a couple of good dogs it might have been a close thing."

Dan Craig nodded. "A good cougar dog's worth money in this neck of the woods," he put in. "Remember the story old John Huelsdonk used to tell—about the time that she-bear knocked him down? He always said his dog Tom saved his life. Tom sailed in and tackled the bear before she could finish off the old man. Gave him a chance to roll over and reach his rifle. After that it didn't take long. He killed her with one shot."

"He was a pretty rugged citizen," Campbell chuckled. "Wish you could have met old John. He died last October, nearly eighty years old. Folks called him 'the Iron Man of the Hoh,' and he deserved it. Stood 'way over six feet and weighed two hundred and fifteen pounds. He was one of the real pioneers. Strong? He could pack a bigger load than any man in the Olympics. One time he carried an iron cookstove on his back—lugged it the whole twenty-two miles up the Hoh to his house. A ranger met him on the trail and asked him if it wasn't pretty heavy.

" 'Well,' says John, 'I don't mind it so much, only there's a hundred-pound sack o' flour in the oven that keeps shifting around and unsettling the load.' "

When the laughter had subsided, Dick returned to his original subject. "You mean, then, that there aren't any really dangerous animals up here?" he asked.

"No more dangerous than you'd find in a barnyard," the Chief Ranger answered. "You can get kicked by a mule or chased by a bull, if you don't treat 'em with respect. Same way around here. We don't have a single poison snake in the Park. Sure, there are bears, but if you leave her cubs alone even a big old she-bear will stay away from you. Cougars sometimes follow folks along the trail, but that's just cat curiosity. I reckon a bull elk in rutting season is about the meanest animal we can lay claim to. Wouldn't you say so, Dan?"

"I guess so," Craig agreed. "But they mostly take it out on each other. Anyhow, it'll be three more months before they begin to get ornery, and you'll be back home in Washington, D. C."

By nine o'clock everybody was ready for bed.

"I'll give you a call around six," said Craig as he bade them good night. "We ought to be packed and ready to go by seven."

Dick's cot was comfortable enough, but his mind was so filled with new impressions that it took him a little time to go to sleep. The knock on his door at dawn woke him from deep slumber, and for a moment he couldn't remember where he was. Then, in the dim light, he saw the rough surface of the fir slabs that formed the partition and his head cleared. He jumped out of bed and into his clothes in a hurry.

Fong Yee must have been up still earlier, for there was a good breakfast waiting for the travelers in the main room of the camp. Well before seven Craig helped them adjust their packs, gave a last check to their equipment, and led the way out into the morning mist.

"This'll clear in another half hour," he said, "but we may as well start. There's a good trail the first few miles."

The fog, seeping up from the canyon bottom, was tinged with gold by the sun, which had now risen above the rim of hills to the east. They went in single file along a well-marked footpath. The river brawled over rocks, hundreds of feet below them. Squirrels raced through the limbs overhead and Oregon jays clucked and chatted in the brush.

The pack rode comfortably on Dick's back and shoulders. He felt strong and fresh. It was hard to believe he was carrying fifty pounds.

"We're lucky to have a made trail along here," Craig told them. "These deep river valleys are wicked when you have to break trail. There are thickets of vine maple and buck brush, and worst of all there's devil's club. It's got sharp spikes all over it—even on the leaves. Then if you try to follow the stream bed you're likely to get into gorges where the rocks go up fifty or sixty feet, straight as the wall of a house. That's why we've built our trails up along the mountainsides."

The fog lifted gradually. First they could see far up into the dark timber across the valley. Then, through the vanishing wreaths of mist a lofty peak glinted in the sun. They were climbing now, on a narrow, difficult path that clung to the sheer side of the mountain. It doubled on itself in ladder-like switchbacks. At the end of another hour they must have gained seven or eight hundred feet of elevation, for the sound of the river was lost in the depths of the canyon below them. At the top of an extra steep climb, Craig paused for a breather.

"Sit down here on the ledge," he said. "You'll find the bottom of your pack-board is just long enough to take the weight off your shoulders."

"Whew!" Dr. Randolph grinned, mopping his forehead. "Makes me short of breath."

"Well, we've come up pretty fast," said the ranger. "We're up around twenty-five hundred feet here to cross this spur. Have to go down again on the other side before we can start our real climbing. That'll come tomorrow."

Dick glanced at his father and saw that he was already absorbed in studying the leaves and petals of a tiny flower, growing out of a crevice in the rock. He knew then that the little scientist was going to be all right.

Their perch on the mountainside gave them a splendid view down both sides of the spur. Just opposite them, a hurrying stream tumbled in a slim, hundred-foot waterfall into the river valley. At the foot of the cataract there was a pool, half hidden by brush and trees. As Dick looked down at it he saw a movement in the shadows beside the pool. A black-tail doe stepped daintily out on the bank, cocked her great ears to listen for a moment, then bent her head swiftly to drink.

"See the fawn with her?" Craig whispered. "Just back there in the bushes—his spots blend in with the leaves."

Dick stared eagerly, but it wasn't until the doe finished her drink and slipped back into the cover that he made out the shape of the moving fawn.

"The deer stay down here all summer," said the ranger. "But most of the elk move up to the high meadows. The bulls don't like the woods when their antlers are in velvet. Those soft horns hurt if they get bumped by a branch, I guess."

After a twenty-minute rest they got up again, settling their packs. The trail dipped sharply into a broad ravine beyond the spur, angling down in another series of switchbacks. Here, where the slopes were not quite so steep, Dick saw such timber as he had never dreamed of. There were Douglas fir and Western hemlock and the giant canoe cedars from which the Indians had made their totem poles and war canoes through the centuries. Primeval trees of monstrous girth stood shoulder to shoulder along the mountainside, acre after acre, their feathery tops a full two hundred feet above the earth. Between their soaring pillars only an occasional shaft of sunlight filtered down, touching the green of ferns and the velvety brown of fallen needles. The boy felt reverent, as if he were in church—a vast, hushed, softly lighted church, nobler than any built by man.

Craig's voice broke the spell. "Trail goes over a stream down here a way," he called over his shoulder. "You'll have your first log bridge to cross."

In a few more minutes they caught sight of it. A huge hemlock had fallen across the chasm, its roots still thrusting into the air from the slope just below them. The broken top was buried in the opposite hillside, eighty feet away.

The ranger clambered up between the roots and gave a hand first to Dr. Randolph, then to Dick. When they were all standing on the huge trunk he turned and set off toward the farther end.

"Nothing to worry about," he called. "It'll shake a little, but it's solid."

They could feel the big log vibrate to the tread of Craig's feet. When the ranger was safely over, Dick started. There was more spring to the trunk than he had expected and he had a sudden sense of panic as he saw the rocky stream bed a hundred feet below him. He broke his stride for a moment to steady himself, then walked ahead, his eyes resolutely on the center of the log in front of him.

It was only when he stepped off at the other end that he realized he had been holding his breath most of the way over. The sight of his father, crossing calmly behind him, made the boy ashamed of himself.

They began climbing once more, bearing to the left along the face of the main canyon. Craig kept his eye on them, watching for signs of fatigue, but neither Dick nor his father had yet begun to feel really tired. Even so, they were glad when noon came and they could set down their packs and stretch their arms.

The ranger made a quick fire on a rocky ledge and brought water from a near-by spring to make tea. Then while they munched the sandwiches they had tucked in the tops of their packs they settled back for a comfortable hour of rest and talk.

"This Four Lakes Basin where we're going," said Dick, "has anybody been up there lately—this summer, I mean?"

"Well," the ranger answered, "I've stopped in a couple of times, but no campers have been up—that is—I—"

He hesitated a moment, flushing under his tan. "Didn't the Chief say anything about it?"

Dr. Randolph's eyebrows lifted behind his spectacles. "About what?" he asked mildly.

"Nothing, really, I guess—only—well, last March,

when I made my first trip up above timberline, I found what looked like ski tracks. Couldn't be sure, because there'd been three or four inches of snow the night before. But there they were leading across the drifts and up to a notch between two peaks. I followed 'em a mile or more, right to the edge of a fifty-foot cliff. And there they disappeared. The queer part of it was that not a soul had gone up our side of the mountains since the first snow, last November. And mighty few people have ever crossed the Olympics in winter. The Chief thought I'd dreamed it—until a couple of months later. He was up on the trail to Constance Pass and found a broken ski. He's still got it, down at camp. Funniest-looking ski you ever saw—looks as if it had been whittled out with a jackknife. There's a slot burned through it, and a piece of raw elk-hide, with the hair on, running through the slot for a strap. We figured at first some Boy Scout had made it, but killing elk in a National Park isn't the sort of thing they do."

Dr. Randolph chuckled. "So you've got a little mystery on your hands," he said. "I suppose there's some very simple explanation. If we run across any more clues up there we'll let you know."

"Do the Scouts do much camping in the Olympics?" Dick asked.

"They've got a good-sized summer camp down on the Hood Canal," said Craig. "But only the huskiest boys and the best woodsmen get up into the mountains. Matter of fact that was my first experience in this section. There were twelve of us, all picked Scout Rangers, and we sure did some tough climbing in those two weeks. You know quite a few of the peaks and streams were first explored and named by Scout troops from Seattle."

He stood up, stretched, and looked aloft at the sky.

"Clouding up a little," he said. "Might get rain before night, and if we do I'd like to reach the shelter first. Let's get those packs on."

Four

THE CLOUDS THICKENED, STREAMING IN gray vapor past the high white peaks. Little rain squalls obscured the timbered valleys ahead and occasionally a few drops fell on the heads of the three who trudged steadily up the canyon trail.

Dick's knees and legs were tired, and he had long since discovered that a fifty-pound pack was a heavy load. He could see lines of weariness in his father's face, too, but the wiry little scientist made no complaint.

There were more log bridges to cross, more steep scrambles up and down the sides of ravines. Just when it seemed that the day's journey would never end, their ranger guide paused and gestured ahead with his arm.

"We made it," he called cheerfully. "There's the lean-to, and we didn't get wet, to speak of."

They found themselves on a tiny natural plateau, a dozen yards wide, perched halfway up the mountainside. The shelter was built of poles, and roofed with big, hand-split cedar shakes. Its open side faced toward the canyon. The huge, charred log that lay across the front of the lean-to bore evidence of many campfires.

Dick set down his pack and followed Craig in a search for firewood. Down the slope a few yards there was a broken stump, the remains of a big tree that had blown down years before. The ranger had his ax out and began splitting off chunks of the dry wood. When they had as much as they could carry, they climbed back to the shelf of ground above and stacked the fuel under the lean-to.

The ranger's fire-building technique was simple and efficient. Dick watched every move, for he knew he would be responsible for the same job when they reached the high meadows. Craig chose five or six pieces of kindling, whittled a fringe of shavings near the end of each, and set them tent-fashion against the backlog. A handful of small twigs and dry needles was laid just under the shavings and a single match sufficed to start a healthy flame. In a minute or two the fire was going nicely, despite the light rain that had begun to fall.

Before darkness settled over the canyon they had cooked and eaten supper, pulled a few fir tips to lay on the dry floor of the shelter, and spread their sleeping bags. The rain increased and puffs of wind swayed the big trees above. They sat comfortably, facing the sputtering blaze, and Craig leaned back, stretching luxuriously.

"How'd those packs ride?" he asked.

Dr. Randolph smiled and rubbed the small of his back. "They didn't get any lighter on the trip," he said.

"That's to be expected," the ranger chuckled. "You'll find it easier tomorrow, just so there's no chafing on your shoulders. Packing is something you get used to after a while. Remember old John Huelsdonk, the 'Iron Man of the Hoh' we were telling you about? There's another story about him I always liked.

"Around thirty years ago they began building roads up into the mountains from the coast. All the supplies had to be packed in for the crews, and a lot of young huskies got good pay for lugging a hundred-pound pack up the trail. Pa Huelsdonk had been hurt in a logging accident and wasn't in the best of shape, but he asked if he could help. Well, sir, as long as the job lasted the old man carried *two* of those big packs every trip. He wasn't showing off, either. Did it because he needed the money. You see, he was putting his four girls through college."

"Gosh!" Dick murmured. "What a man he must have

been!"

"Yes, he was a man," said Craig, "and he had a heart as big as his body. Hated cougars like poison because they killed so many elk. He never could keep count of all the cats he killed, but it was in the hundreds. Then when he'd reduced the cougar population, he found the elk were multiplying too fast and starving to death. He'd upset the balance of Nature. After that he used to go out and find young elk calves that were sick or hungry and carry them home in his arms. When he'd nursed them until they were strong he sent them to zoos and protected herds. Yep, this country's going to miss Pa Huelsdonk."

Before bedtime he told them other stories—of the long wars between the Quillayute Indians and the fierce Makah tribe to the north—of the fleets of big war canoes loaded with braves that raided along the coast and burned the villages before the white men came.

By eight-thirty Dick and his father were having a hard time keeping their eyes open and were glad to crawl into their sleeping bags. The rain continued falling, and the wind thrashed and moaned in the fir-tops, but Dick scarcely heard them. He was asleep in a few seconds.

Some time in the middle of the night he woke to the sound of a sudden, earth-shaking crash. Lifting himself on one elbow he stared out into the wet darkness. The fire had long since gone out and the night was pitch black.

Craig's voice came, quiet and reassuring. "Big tree falling," he said. "Nothing to worry about. I figure the storm's about over."

The boy snuggled down into his eiderdown and was soon asleep again. When next he opened his eyes, the first gray of dawn had reached down into the canyon. Craig was up and building a fire, and the rain had stopped.

"Rise and shine!" cried the ranger. "Breakfast'll be ready before you know it, and there's a fine, clear day coming up."

There was a spring tumbling out of the rocks a few yards beyond the lean-to. Dick walked over to it, stretching his arms and legs to get the stiffness out of his muscles, and doused his face in the icy water. He brushed his teeth, ran a comb through his hair and sniffed the breeze. Mingled with the scent of wood smoke was a tantalizing aroma of frying bacon. He discovered suddenly that he was ravenously hungry.

It was less than an hour later that they hit the trail once more. Half a mile up the valley Craig swung to the right, along the side of a small branch canyon. There was no longer any well-marked path. The ranger followed blazes he had cut in the tree trunks on earlier expeditions.

They had to climb over windfalls and claw their way through brush in many places. Coming around a bend in the canyon wall they saw a lofty waterfall some distance ahead, and the trail went up more steeply, angling toward the heights from which the cataract sprang.

The last few hundred yards were the toughest going they had yet encountered. They were up beyond the firs now, but scattered mountain hemlocks clung to the rocky slope. For half an hour the climbers sweated it out, searching for footholds, pulling themselves upward by roots and down-hanging limbs.

At last they were above the waterfall and could look down along its dizzy drop to the depths of the ravine, hundreds of feet below. A cloud of mist hung above the tumbling water, catching the sun in a vivid rainbow. The roar of the cataract was so loud in their ears that they had to shout to make themselves heard.

"Mighty near as pretty as Yosemite," Craig bellowed. "Yet I don't suppose fifty people besides ourselves have ever seen it!"

"Hey!" Dick yelled in answer. "Let me go off a little way where I can get a picture. I won't be long."

He slipped out of the pack straps and hurried back along the side of the canyon, all his weariness forgotten. In a few moments he found a perch on an outcrop of rock where his view commanded the whole height of the fall. He unlimbered his camera, set the adjustments and put his eye to the finder. The early light was over his right shoulder, for he was looking straight north.

The picture he saw was so exciting that he had to wait and take a deep breath to steady his hands. He clicked the shutter, moved a few yards to another position and tried another shot. Just for safety he took two more before he returned to join the other members of the party.

"Think you got it?" asked the ranger.

"I'm pretty sure I did—and, boy! what a kodachrome it'll make!"

"Well," said Craig, "we'd better start along. We've still got a long way to go, but you'll find this next stretch is easier."

Above the falls the valley widened out in more gentle slopes. Long ago there had been a forest fire in this basin. A few stark, blackened tree stubs still rose here and there, but most of the valley was filled with a sea of huckleberry bushes. Craig chose a narrow, twisting game trail that threaded the brush along the eastern side of the valley. He pointed to abundant elk sign as they followed the trail, and once he stopped to show them a little mound of dirt, piled up neatly in the middle of the path.

"Cougars do that," he explained. "No reason for it that anybody knows. Just playfulness, I guess—a sign that says 'Kilroy was here.'"

They had covered more than half the length of the basin when Craig paused, silently lifting his hand in warning. The breeze was blowing toward them from the north. A hundred yards ahead they saw a movement among the waist-high berry bushes—a rusty-black bulk that stirred the leaves and twigs.

"Bear," whispered the ranger. "Doesn't smell us yet."

Dick and his father tiptoed forward, following in Craig's careful footsteps. They had approached near enough to hear the bear snuffling and munching on the succulent fruit before he was aware of their presence. Then some scent or sound must have reached the big animal. He reared up suddenly, testing the air with his wrinkled nose, looked in their direction for a startled second, then dropped on all fours and raced away downhill like a runaway locomotive.

Dick had been holding his camera ready, but the bear was gone before he could locate him in the finder.

"Darn!" he growled. "A swell shot and I missed it!"

Craig laughed. "You'd have had to be faster'n chain lightning to catch that one," said he. "Pretty good-sized bear. I reckon he'd weigh around four hundred pounds. When he stood up he was taller than most men and built like a barrel."

As they neared the upper end of the valley, Dick took an extra hitch in his belt and settled his pack firmly. The head wall went up at an angle of more than forty-five degrees and looked forbiddingly rough and rocky.

It took them two hours of steady climbing, with only one brief rest, to reach the top. But the view they found up there was worth all their toil.

Opening out ahead rose peak after white-robed peak— a seemingly endless parade of mountains that made Dick think of the crowding crests of waves in a northeast storm. Again he whipped out his camera and started taking pictures.

Craig laughed. "I wouldn't waste too much film on

this," he said. "You'll find better chances when you get up higher. We're only about four thousand feet here."

"Well," said Dick, "maybe you're right, but it's hard to keep your camera in the case when you see something like this. Is that Mt. Olympus—the high one up there?"

"No, you won't see Olympus for a while yet. It's nearly thirty miles west of here. That big peak is Mt. Deception, with the Needles showing up over its shoulder. Deception's no slouch of a mountain, though. It's pretty close to eight thousand feet, and Olympus itself is only eighty-one hundred. That's what makes these mountains different from any others in the world. There are forty or fifty peaks, all about the same size and all jammed together like a herd of cattle."

They went forward again, following a narrow rocky ridge that led upward between thickets of mountain hemlock and Engleman spruce. As they gained another few hundred feet of altitude, even these hardy evergreens gave way to bare slopes where only a few stunted, wind-twisted hemlocks clung to the crevices.

Over on the opposite mountainside the sun glinted on a huge fan-shaped sheet of ice, funneling down from a lofty ravine, and Dick paused, gaping at the shimmering, green-white mass.

"I guess that's our first glacier," said Dr. Randolph.

"Right." Craig nodded. "You'll find more of them up above, but that's a pretty fair sample. The Olympics are full of small glaciers. What happens is that the snow packs down hundreds of feet deep in those high valleys in the winter. The weight of it keeps pushing ice out at the foot, and there's so much that the sun can't melt it till it spreads out thin."

They ate their lunch on a broad, slanting ledge where the rock "cleaver" they had been climbing joined the wall of the mountain.

Dick finished his meal and sat resting against the packboard. His glance roved along the mountainside.

"It's queer," he said, "but I can't find a sign of a trail going on from here."

Craig grinned. "It doesn't exactly go on," he replied. "It goes up—what there is of it." And he jerked a thumb toward the crag above them.

Dr. Randolph, following the gesture with his eye, got up and settled the pack on his shoulders. "If that's the case," he remarked drily, "I think we'd better get at it."

Dick, too, took an appraising look at the cliff and moved his camera around to the side of his belt. He had a hunch there would be places up there where he wouldn't want anything bulky between himself and the rock.

Craig led the way. They had no ropes, no alpenstocks or crampons, but foot by foot they scaled the almost perpendicular face of the crag. It was a matter of finding toeholds and places where fingers could grip—of edging carefully along narrow shelves—of clinging like leeches to the rock wall. Dick didn't dare look down. He concentrated on the next yard or two above him, following the sure movements of the ranger and his father. He was beginning to have a brand-new kind of respect for the quiet little botanist.

After what seemed an endless time he felt a strong hand grip his lifted wrist, and a moment later he was being hauled over the top.

"Good boy!" said Dan Craig. "I'm proud of both of you. This was the only place that had me worried and you made it fine. As for your dad, I take my hat off to a game guy!"

Easing over on his side, Dick looked at the small, bespectacled man who sat panting beside him, and a lump came in his throat.

"Me, too," he said.

Five

FROM THE TOP OF THE CLIFF THEY COULD
look back over much of the country they had traveled
through. There were the shaggy foothills and deep, timbered valleys, the broad, green mat of blueberry thickets
and the sparkling cone of the glacier. And higher, to the
north, south, east and west, the jagged crests of mountains.

All three of them sat silent for a little while, drinking

in that grandeur. It was Craig who spoke first.

"When I'm alone up here," he said quietly, "I keep trying to remember a line of poetry—from Kipling, I think. It's about how the mountains pull you—make you want to see what's on the other side. The only words I'm sure of are 'behind the ranges.' Do you know how the rest goes?"

Dr. Randolph nodded. "It's one of my favorites, too," he said.

> " 'Something hidden—go and find it!
> Go and look behind the ranges—
> Something lost behind the ranges;
> Lost, and waiting for you—go!'

"It's Kipling, all right—a poem called *The Explorers.*"

Craig repeated the verse over to himself. "Gee," he murmured. "That really talks to you, doesn't it? Makes your skin tingle and your feet get restless. And that reminds me—the place we're headed for is behind a couple more ranges, so we'd better start those feet moving."

Once more they got up and settled their packs. Dick no longer felt tired or shaky. He was eager to get on with the journey. Above the cliff stretched a long hogback, slanting upward to a saddle between two rugged peaks. They climbed through scattered timber, picking their way around outcroppings of rock. There was no marked trail.

Craig led the way, keeping his direction by landmarks and the slope of the ground. After two hours of it they halted for a breathing spell.

"If we can get up to the saddle before sunset," said the ranger, "I think I can show you something pretty."

Dick made a guess. "You mean that's Four Lakes Basin, just beyond the saddle?" he asked.

"You're trying to get there too fast," Craig chuckled. "No, your basin is higher still, half a day's hike from the place we'll stop tonight."

He wouldn't tell them any more, but he had aroused Dick's curiosity and the boy pushed on with new energy. The sun was just touching the summits of a cluster of high mountains to the west when they toiled up the last few hundred yards to the top of the pass.

There was a gnarled old mountain hemlock overhanging a ledge near the saddle's crest.

"That's all the shelter we'll have for tonight," said Craig. "I've slept here before and it isn't bad. Let's leave our packs under the tree and do a little exploring before it gets dark.

He motioned to them to go quietly and moved ahead to a spot that commanded a view of the country beyond. There at their feet spread a great meadow, dotted with clumps of low, dark alpine fir. And grazing in the lush grass, a quarter of a mile to the north, was a herd of elk.

"Sh," Craig warned. "That's what I wanted you to see. Maybe we can get closer if we don't make any noise. Follow me."

Dick's heart pounded with excitement as he ducked

low, creeping down through the brush and tall grass. They made a circuit to the north, crawling on their bellies when they had to cross open spaces, and keeping down-wind from the herd.

Each time Dick caught a glimpse of the animals he grew more excited. Used to deer, he was surprised at their size. Even the cow elk looked as big as horses. And more impressive still were the bulls, standing on guard with their huge, velvet-covered antlers lifted high. There were gangling calves, too, nuzzling at their mothers or chewing on the tender grass.

The stalkers had crept almost within a stone's throw of the herd when one of the bulls must have caught their scent. At his loud snort of warning, all the elk in the meadow raised their heads, motionless as statues except for the nervous stirring of their great ears. Then, with another snort, the bull drove the herd off before him at a quick trot. As the brown bodies swung away, the big, round patch on the rump of each showed up in pale straw-color, like the sudden flash of a full moon.

Dick got his camera out of its case as quickly as he could, but the light was too bad and the elk too far away for a successful picture.

"Boy!" he exclaimed. "Wasn't that a sight? Do you think they'll still be here in the morning? I'd give a lot if I could get a good color shot."

"Don't believe they'll run far," Craig told him. "If it

had been cougar they smelled, they might decide to change their pasture. But they're getting pretty tame as far as men are concerned. I imagine you'll get another chance for a picture tomorrow."

They walked back up the hill to the place where they had left their packs. There was a dead stub close by, and the ranger quickly chopped out enough dry wood for a supper fire. This time he let Dick build and light it.

"Just want to make sure you folks won't starve to death when you're on your own," he grinned. "I reckon you'll make out all right. Now let's see how you do with the cooking."

He complimented the boy on the meal he prepared. Water for the tea had to be carried from a spring down in the meadow, and Dick returned to it in the gathering darkness to wash up the pans. He was stooping above the tiny pool, when he heard a crackle of brush in the fir thicket twenty yards beyond him. Something was running away—not in animal leaps but with a muffled thud of feet that sounded strangely human.

"Hey!" yelled the startled boy. "Who's there?"

There was no answer, and the footsteps were lost now in the vast silence of the mountain night.

Dick gave the utensils a hasty rinse and started back toward the small, flickering dot of light that showed where the campfire was. Once or twice he looked back over his shoulder, but in the blackness that lay over the meadow he could see nothing.

"Who were you hollering at?" asked Craig, when the boy rejoined his companions. "Didn't think there were any folks up here, did you?"

"I didn't," Dick answered, somewhat embarrassed. "But after what I heard I'm not so sure. It was the darnedest thing—sounded exactly like a man running."

The ranger laughed. "No," he said, "I guess we'll have to count that one out. Might have been one o' those bull elk. They're curious, you know. Perhaps he saw the fire and came to sniff around a little. Or he might have been coming to the spring for a drink. When you scared him, he trotted off."

"Maybe that was it," Dick agreed. He wasn't wholly convinced, but he had to admit he knew very little about elk.

The fire was dying and the evening was rapidly growing chilly. They were glad to crawl into their sleeping bags, even though the bare ledge made a hard bed.

"We might have camped down there in the meadow where the ground's softer," said Craig. "But I sort of like this old hemlock for a roof."

Dick made no answer, but he was glad, at that moment, not to be sleeping in the meadow. He lay on his back, staring up through the gently stirring boughs of the tree. There were openings up there through which the stars glittered frostily. He watched them as long as his eyes would stay open, then drifted into dreamless sleep.

.   .   .

The sound of Craig's voice, cheerfully raised in song, woke the boy next morning.

"Throw another log on the fire," warbled the ranger, and a crackle of burning wood announced that he was suiting his action to the words.

Dick crawled out of his eiderdown, pulled on his boots and looked about him. A gray shroud of fog hung in the pass. It was impossible to see more than a hundred feet in any direction.

"Gosh," he said, disappointed. "I hoped to get a shot of those elk this morning."

"Don't give up hoping," Craig replied. "Generally these morning mists lift or burn off pretty early. How about getting me some water for breakfast?"

The boy picked up the largest stewpan and scrambled downhill to the spring in the meadow. In the fog it took him a little time to find the place. After casting back and forth a few times he came on it suddenly, and the first thing he saw was a hand-print in the mud at one side of the little pool.

Had he made it himself, when he was here last night? He couldn't remember putting his hand palm down in the muck. Nor did the blurred print look like his own. Studying it more carefully he was startled to see that the mark made by the forefinger ended at the second joint. He held his own left hand above the print and made the further discovery that the outline in the mud was both longer and broader.

HE HELD HIS OWN LEFT HAND ABOVE THE PRINT

Excited, he filled the pan with water and went quickly back to camp.

"Well," he told the others, "I've found something that makes me think I was right about hearing a man running away last night."

He described the hand-print, and as he talked Craig's forehead wrinkled in puzzlement.

"That's mighty strange," said the ranger. "Of course it's possible there's somebody camping up here, but if so, why wouldn't he come in and say 'Howdy' when he heard you call to him? All I can figure is that it's some kind of poacher who doesn't want to be seen. Once in a while an Indian will act that way, but they always stay down in the thick timber. There's something about the high country they don't like—a kind of tribal superstition left over from the old times. They used to think there were cruel gods living up in the peaks. Let's eat breakfast and get started. I'd like to take a look at this print you found."

The fog was beginning to break when they reached the spring. For several minutes the ranger and Dr. Randolph examined the mark in the mud. Then Craig stood up and scratched his head.

"No mistake about that," said he. "Left hand, with one finger gone at the joint. I'll have to do a little investigating this afternoon on my way down. If I don't find the fellow I'll report this to the Chief as soon as I get to a phone box."

They moved on across the mile-wide meadow. As the

mists lifted they could see a high ridge ahead, with patches of snow among the rocks.

"That's the east wall of your basin," Craig told them. "Not as tough a climb as it looks from here. We ought to make it by noon or a little after."

The morning sun broke through the clouds a few minutes later, and just as it flooded the meadow Dick saw a magnificent bull elk step out of a fir thicket barely fifty yards away. His father and the ranger caught sight of the animal at the same moment and stopped, motionless. With fumbling fingers, Dick got his camera out. There was no time to make any calculations or settings. He stole a quick glance to assure himself the bull was still there, then fixed his eyes on the finder.

The big elk stood as if posing for a portrait. His antlers were held proudly aloft, and his dark brown ruff contrasted beautifully with the lighter tan of his sides. He waited just long enough for the boy to press the shutter, then turned disdainfully and vanished among the fir boughs.

"Whew!" breathed Dick. "That was close but I got him. Everything broke just right. I even had it set for the right distance, by dumb luck."

"Good," said Craig. "Let's be on our way."

The snowy ridge seemed to be as far away as ever when they reached the upper end of the meadow. The approach to it lay up a long spur of rocky ground. It was bare of vegetation except for a few stunted evergreens and tufts of hardy grass.

"We're about a mile above sea level here," the ranger remarked, as they panted up the slope. "By the time we get to the top of the ridge we'll have climbed another thousand feet, so take it steady and easy."

Without the prospect of new discoveries beyond the beckoning mountain wall, Dick would have found it a dull morning's work. They went constantly upward, but never in a straight line. There were cliffs and rough spots around which they contoured, following faintly marked game trails. For generations the elk must have used this route to reach their summer pasture in the high basins.

The sun beat down brightly, and the sweat ran into Dick's eyes. He had become fairly used to the weight of the pack by now, but it had begun to feel very heavy before they reached the last steep climb to the summit. There at the foot of the snow slide they rested for a few minutes.

Dr. Randolph took off his hat and mopped his forehead.

"Surprising how tired you can get in this thin air," he said apologetically. "But there's one thing about it— now that we're up here the trip down will be easier."

Craig looked at his watch. "Half an hour to noon," he told them. "We'll save lunch till we're over the hump. Ready to tackle the slide? Watch your footing. It may be pretty slippery."

There was a thick crust of ice on the snow, and Dick

found he had to plant his feet solidly at each step, letting the sharp triconi nails take hold. The slide went up at a sharp angle, steep and smooth as the roof of a house. They climbed slowly but steadily for twenty minutes. Then the boy heard a triumphant hail from Craig, up in the lead, and in a few more strides he joined the others on the crest.

For the first moment both he and his father were speechless. Then the botanist found breath enough to voice his thoughts.

"Glorious!" he murmured reverently. "This is what I came to find. Ten billion flowers in bloom!"

Six

THE BASIN WAS THREE OR FOUR MILES
across, a vast, flat-bottomed bowl, ringed by snowy peaks
and ridges. In the middle distance glimmered the surface
of a little lake, bluer than the sky itself. Other sheets of
water were visible, away toward the farther rim, and here
and there Dick could see the twisted trunks and branches
of dwarf evergreens. But the greater part of the basin's
floor was covered by a solid carpet of tiny flowering

plants. They seemed to be of every color in the spectrum, though pale blue, pink and lavender blooms shading to clear white were the most numerous. Wild bees hummed busily from flower to flower in the bright, still air.

Dr. Randolph hurried down the slope and dropped to his knees in the middle of a bed of low-growing blossoms, his pack still on his back. At that moment Dick heard a high, piercing whistle from the rocks a short distance away. He looked up, startled, and Craig laughed.

"You wanted marmots," he said. "Well, that was one of 'em, saying 'hello.' Listen, now."

From far and near around the basin came a chorus of answering whistles in various pitches.

Dick chuckled. "Sounds like a bunch of kids calling a dog," he said. "But where are they? I don't see a single marmot."

"The one close by here, that gave the first warning, is probably down in his hole, with just his nose sticking out. He'll wait to see if we're dangerous before he comes out again."

They followed the botanist down the hill and found him so deeply absorbed they had to call him twice before he looked up.

"Oh, yes—sorry," he told the ranger with a smile. "You want to eat some lunch and start down, don't you? All right, I'll be along in a moment."

Dick followed Craig down the meadow to the edge of the first lake and set down his pack. A gnarled, dead tree-stub nearby furnished wood for a fire. They made tea, ate some biscuits and chocolate and talked a few minutes while the ranger puffed at his pipe.

"You'll find this about as good a camp site as any," he told the Randolphs. "There isn't much shelter up here, so you'll have to sleep in the open. Those waterproof sleeping bags will help. You'll find enough wood, I reckon, and there's plenty of water. Here's some extra grub I packed for you."

He pulled out a bulky bundle wrapped in a waterproof cover and laid it in the heather beside them.

"I'll be swinging back this way in about a week and I'll drop in to see how you've made out. Lots of luck with the plants and the marmots!"

He grinned a farewell and went off at his long, woodsman's stride toward the place where they had crossed the rim. Dick watched till the distant figure was silhouetted on the skyline. He saw the ranger wave an arm and disappear.

"Well, Dad," he said, "I guess we're on our own. What's first on the program?"

The little scientist looked about vaguely. "I'd like to get back to my specimens," he said. "But it might be a good idea to gather a supply of wood and make some kind of shelter where we can store our food and spare clothes."

"Right," Dick agreed, jumping to his feet. "You go ahead and study your plants. I'll take care of fixing up the camp."

He took the small camp ax and walked north along the shore of the lake toward a clump of half a dozen stunted spruce trees. The meadow sloped gently down to the water. Once he crossed an old game trail and saw the tracks of elk in the soft ground close to the lake's edge.

The sound of his ax rang loud in the stillness as he chopped away at one of the dead spruces. The trunk was a foot through near the base, though the whole height of the tree was scarcely twenty feet. He found the wood hard to cut, and when he finally brought the tree down he saw the reason. The growth rings in the stump were so close together he could hardly count them. The spruce had been fighting the mountain winds, deep snows and cold for more than eighty winters, yet it was still a dwarf in size.

Dick cut the heavy trunk into two lengths and started to drag one of them back to the place where their duffel lay. Then he changed his mind. The clump of trees would give a little shelter and a supply of fuel. Why not move their camp over here? He made two trips, carrying the packs, and set about building a fireplace from the loose stones that lay among the heather. When that was completed he went to work on a cuddy for their supplies. Choosing a stout crotch about as high as his head in one of the trees, he floored it with a platform of limbs and twigs, braced an inverted "V" of sticks above, and tied over them the small tarpaulin that Craig had used to wrap the extra provisions. It made a serviceable cupboard, big enough to hold their supplies and fairly weather-tight.

Next the boy split up the dead spruce, piling the wood between two trees. In an hour he had what looked like enough for several days. With everything tucked away shipshape, the camp had a businesslike appearance that pleased him.

But it was too fine a day to stand there admiring his handiwork. There were so many other things to see and do that he had a hard time choosing. The hot sun beating down on his back reminded him that a bath and a change of clothes were in order. He hadn't undressed since leaving the Ranger Station, three days before. With a thrill of anticipation he stripped and ran down to the lake.

The water was clear as crystal, and he could see the rocky bottom, sloping steeply away from the shore. When he tested its temperature with a toe it felt surprisingly warm.

"Here goes!" he cried exultantly, and took off in a long, shallow dive. The next instant he was clawing his way back to the surface with frantic strokes. A mountain lake, he had discovered, could be deceptively comfortable on top, and cold as arctic ice three feet down. He floated for a while, paddling to keep himself in the sun-warmed upper layer of water, and scrubbed his body clean.

It was an exhilarating experience, swimming there among the peaks of the high wilderness, where perhaps no human being had ever bathed before. When he stepped out into the thin, sunny air he was dry before he had gone a dozen yards.

"Boy!" he said to himself, "why wear any clothes, if it's going to be as warm as this?"

He pulled on a pair of shorts and the light moccasins he had brought in his pack, picked up his camera and set off on an exploring trip down the meadow.

It was impossible to avoid stepping on the little blossoms that covered the ground. At first he felt like a trespasser in some fabulous garden, but after a time he forgot the flowers and kept his eyes on the crags and crests and snow slides that ringed the basin.

The lake in which he had bathed had its outlet in a gently flowing little stream that meandered through the meadows. After perhaps half a mile it emptied into a second pond and thence, Dick assumed, into the third and fourth, beyond. He could see a narrow gap in the mountain wall at the farther end of the basin. There, Craig had told him, the headwaters of Greywolf River left the high valley in a hundred-foot plunge and went cascading down the mountains to join the Dungeness, flowing north to the Strait of Juan de Fuca.

The boy jumped the outlet brook and made his way across the basin. There was a great, rough spur of rock over on that side that looked interesting. It thrust out several hundred yards from the main ridge, and its crest was broken by deep, irregular crevices.

66

He thought it might be a good place for marmots, and his guess was proved right as he drew nearer. Whistles, clear and sharp, greeted his approach. He walked slowly, shading his eyes and searching the rocky surface of the outcrop. At last he saw a movement. A furry, brownish animal a little larger than an ordinary house cat galloped a few yards on its short legs, then sat erect and uttered one of those shrill, cheerful whistles.

Dick stood perfectly still. He was too far away for a camera shot and he didn't want to frighten the animal into its burrow. After a moment he caught sight of another marmot, higher up the rocks. As he watched he realized that the whole slope was dotted with them, though their gray-brown fur made them practically invisible until they moved.

Apparently they had decided he was harmless, for they went unconcernedly about their business. Some, he could see, were stretched out, sunning themselves in front of their holes. Others nibbled at scattered patches of alpine grass that clung to the crannies of the rocks. By good luck he seemed to have discovered a sort of marmot castle.

After a while he focused the camera and raised it slowly. The craggy spur, with its backdrop of snow-covered peaks and the blanket of mountain flowers at its foot, would make an ideal setting for a natural history group in the museum. He took several pictures, then closed the camera and stepped cautiously nearer. In an instant the marmot fortress was on the alert. Whistles echoed back and forth around the spur. Before he could take three strides every one of the plump beasts had dived below ground.

Dick grinned to himself. He would have to find some less conspicuous way of stalking these sharp-eyed whistlers. But at least he knew where to come when he wanted to study them.

For another two hours he wandered along the edges of the meadow, with the friendly sun beating on his bare shoulders and chest. Then a cold wind came down off the snowcaps to the west and he had to run part of the way back to camp to keep warm.

His father was still squatting happily among his flowers, a distant brown dot against the paler, more delicate colors of the meadow. Dick put on some clothes and went to join him.

Dr. Randolph had a wide, shallow specimen-box unfolded beside him, and many of its small compartments were filled.

"Amazing!" he beamed. "I've already found twenty-six species and sub-species, with four or five others that need further checking—and I've hardly stirred from this one spot."

"That's swell," Dick replied. "But it's getting along toward evening. Come on back and take a look at our camp. I've fixed up a pretty good layout, if I do say so myself."

At sunset the marmots gave a few good-night whistles

and retired to their burrows. A steady wind blew, rustling the boughs of the spruces, but otherwise all was silent in the basin. Their voices, and the sound of the ax, seemed extra loud in the wide stillness.

Dick's fireplace drew well and soon they had a pan of bacon sputtering over the flames. As they ate, the boy described his swim and the discovery of the marmot colony.

"They're bigger than I thought," he told his father. "The full-grown ones look half again as big as one of our eastern woodchucks. I'm not sure that little trap I bought will hold 'em. But anyhow I want to study their habits and get some better pictures first."

"That's right," the botanist nodded in approval. "Keep a notebook, too, and describe everything you see. Accurate observation is one of the things a good scientist has to learn. And if you write down your notes on the spot, you're less likely to be accused of exaggerating."

Dick laughed. "That's a little old-fashioned, isn't it, Dad? I'd rather trust a camera, myself. But I'll make a few notes, too."

They finished their meal and walked a short distance along the shadowy meadow. As it grew darker they found themselves stumbling over rocks and hummocks and decided the basin was a poor place for nighttime strolling.

Dick pulled several armfuls of the short-stemmed heather and spread it evenly below the overhanging spruces. Under the sleeping bags the springy stuff made a couch that felt almost luxurious.

"This is pretty nice, eh, Dad?" the boy said drowsily, as he lay there watching the stars. "We're here at last, and everything's perfect. It's almost too good to be true."

It was a moment before Dr. Randolph answered. Then his voice sounded more serious than Dick had expected.

"Yes," he said. "I was thinking the same thing. If I were at all superstitious—which, of course, I'm not, being a scientist—I believe I'd have my fingers crossed."

"Oh, I wouldn't worry," Dick laughed. "There's nothing up here that could possibly spoil our fun except weather, and I guess we can keep pretty snug even in a storm."

The boy yawned and rolled over, reveling in the comfort of his bed and the pleasant weariness of his back and legs. He was still smiling when sleep overtook him.

Seven

THERE WAS LITTLE CHANCE FOR SLUMBER
after dawn in Four Lakes Basin. With the first daylight
the marmots began whistling with such enthusiasm that
their chorus was more effective than any alarm clock.

Dick opened his eyes and stretched. In the brighten-
ing sky that showed through gaps in the spruce top he
could see a few pale stars. It was going to be another
clear day.

He crawled out of the eiderdown into the cold air and

thrashed his arms to work up circulation. By the time he had washed, brought water from the lake and built a fire, he felt like a fighting cock. He started breakfast and called his father.

"You mean you slept right through all that whistling, Dad?" he asked.

"Eh, what's that?" murmured the botanist drowsily. "Whistling? Seems to me I had some sort of dream about a peanut roaster. That must have been it."

Dr. Randolph was eager to get back to his plants, and as soon as the meal was finished he picked up his specimen-box and magnifying glass.

"I'll see you around noontime," Dick called after him. "If you want me I'll be down at that rock spur beyond the first lake."

The boy wore his mountain boots, shorts and a flannel shirt. He slipped a small notebook and pencil in his pocket and strapped the camera to his belt. After a moment's deliberation he decided to take the trap as well. There was a staple on the end of the two-foot chain, and he drove it solidly into the middle of a short log. If, by luck, he should get a marmot in the trap, he didn't want the animal to pull the chain into its burrow.

The sun was just coming over the peaks to the east when he started across the basin. This time, instead of approaching the marmots' citadel from the meadow, he decided to make a circuit along the rim and try to scout them from above.

He found a break in the cliffs, half a mile south of the outcropping spur, and scaled it without too much difficulty. From the crest he could see a magnificent panorama of peaks rising and falling to the west, each with the pink and gold of morning sun on its snowy slopes. He kept just below and behind the ridge, so that his figure wouldn't be exposed on the skyline, and worked his way north, treading carefully on the icy crust.

The country on the outer side of the rim was in striking contrast to the basin itself. The ground dropped away dizzily in snow-covered slopes to a deep canyon below, then went up again in sheer cliffs to the crest of the next ridge. A misstep there, Dick realized, would send him sliding and falling hundreds of feet to the canyon bottom.

It took him twenty or thirty minutes to reach the place he had chosen as an observation post. The crown of the ridge was rougher here, broken by clefts and gullies among the rocks. He crawled up into one of these narrow openings and peered cautiously down upon the marmots' stronghold. For a moment he was disappointed. None of the animals seemed to be in sight. Then, not a dozen feet below him, a dark head popped out of a crevice in the rocks.

It was a full-grown marmot that crept out, inch by inch, to sit in the sun by the door of its burrow. Dick held his breath, careful to make no movement. The marmot's sharp little eyes swept the slope, left, right and down the hill, but never looked directly toward the boy above. It seemed to be satisfied that nothing dangerous was in sight, for it sat up, front paws folded on its stomach, and gave an ear-splitting whistle. Its bushy tail jerked as it made the sound.

Apparently that particular whistle was a sort of all-clear signal. In ten seconds the rocky hill was alive with other marmots. They were of all sizes and all colors, from seal brown to creamy gray. The older ones looked darker about the head and shoulders but were silvery buff on the body and hindquarters. It was the rolypoly marmot pups that took Dick's eye, however. Some were half-grown, others hardly more than eight inches long. They were as comical and full of spirits as miniature bear cubs.

In front of many of the burrows the earth that had been dug out ran downward in a smooth slope, two or three feet high. The boy saw two fat little fellows wrestling at the top of one of these slides. They sat up on their haunches and grasped each other with their paws, mewing and growling like kittens. After a moment's tussling, one lost his balance and went tumbling, heels over head, down the slope. The winner spent no time in gloating but joyfully threw himself down the hill after his defeated rival, rolling like a furry ball. This process was repeated half a dozen times, with first one, then the other of the pups, coming out on top.

As quietly as possible, Dick slipped back out of sight and took his camera out of its case. Then he crawled upward again and trained the lens on the scene below him.

There they were in the finder—the big sentinel marmot directly in the foreground, the wrestling pups twenty feet farther away. He steadied the camera and clicked the shutter.

It made only a tiny sound, but instantly there were sharp, warning whistles and every animal in sight whisked into its burrow.

Delighted as he was to get such a picture, Dick was sorry the show was over. He put away his camera, set the trap and stepped cautiously down into the marmot settlement. Choosing one of the larger holes, he scraped away a little of the earth at its entrance, placed the open trap across the threshold, and sprinkled it with dust and a few blades of grass. Then he went scrambling down the rocks, trying to make as little noise as possible. In a few moments he was back in the meadow once more.

It was only when he looked up the basin toward camp that he remembered his father's advice about taking notes. He sat down on a convenient boulder, pulled out his notebook and pencil and began jotting down some of his observations. At once he realized how little he had really found out about marmots. What did they eat, for instance? He tried to recall more of the scene, but found his attention had been so fully occupied with the young marmots' antics he had noticed very little of what their elders were doing. Somewhat ashamed of himself as a scientist, he resolved to come back and do more observing later on.

Meanwhile it was a perfect morning and he had the whole wide basin to explore.

This time he took a new line, following the foot of the west rim and heading in a northerly direction. Half an hour's hiking brought him to the shore of the third lake. It was bigger in area than either of the upper ones— nearly a mile across, he judged. He was moving along its low bank, looking for elk tracks, when he heard a splash. Out in the water a short distance from shore, he saw a widening ring of ripples.

Dick stood there wondering and watching. The ranger had told him there were no fish in the basin. But surely nothing but a fish could have made that splash. He waited for a minute or two and was about to start on again when a fifteen-inch rainbow trout broke water not a hundred feet away. He could see the glint of sun on its curving side as it arched almost clear of the surface.

Here was a real discovery. Trout in Four Lakes Basin! He had a line and some small hooks in his pack, back at the camping place, though he had not expected to use them. Now, if he could find the right lure, he might be able to surprise his father with something good for supper.

He was tempted to go back for the tackle at once, but there was still a part of the basin he had not seen and the trout would wait.

As he went on he puzzled over Craig's insistence that no fish lived in these waters. The ranger knew his facts about most things, and there were good reasons why he should be right about this. How could native trout get up here in the first place? If the outlet of the basin was a waterfall dropping over a high cliff, it was impossible for any fish to climb it. And Craig had stated positively that the Park Commission had never stocked the lakes.

As he neared the peak at the northwest corner of the basin, a dark speck rose from one of the crags and sailed past on broad wings. It was a bald eagle. The sight of the great bird fired Dick's imagination and suggested an answer to the mystery of the trout. It seemed fantastic enough, but suppose—he told himself—an eagle had seized a spawning fish in one of the streams below and flown with it toward its nest up here in the high peaks. Then suppose the trout had squirmed out of the eagle's claws and fallen into the lake.

The boy laughed at himself. No, that theory was too farfetched. There must be some other watercourse leaving the basin—some route by which trout could find their way into this mile-high valley.

As he went forward his eyes searched the mountain wall for a hidden opening, but there was nothing of the kind. The fourth lake lay close to the northern rim, and he could see a twisting ribbon of water flowing from it toward the deep cleft that formed the basin's only exit. Twenty minutes later he had followed the stream to the foot of the crags.

For a short distance it was possible to enter the chasm

77

by walking along a narrow ledge that hung above the fast-flowing outlet brook. Then the ledge ended abruptly, and the stream bed ran between naked cliffs. From somewhere close ahead came the sound of falling water.

Unable to go any farther, the boy turned back. He was still mystified about the trout, but after all they were there, and he might as well accept the fact and make the most of it.

He made good time on the return trip. It was still an hour before noon when he reached camp and got the fishing tackle out of his pack. His father was half a mile up the meadow and too busy with his botanizing to notice Dick's movements. The boy tied a leader on the line, then went down to the lake's edge and watched the insect life that was skimming above the water. One slim gray fly floated near him and he captured it.

After studying its wing markings, he tried to manufacture an imitation fly out of ravelings from the seam of his wool shirt. It looked fairly satisfactory when he finished tying it, but one cast on the water proved the idea wouldn't work. The wool strands drooped in a wet mass. What he needed was hair and feathers, and he had neither of them at hand.

Dick dug into the shallow soil, looking in vain for worms. Then he chanced to turn over a rock close to the water's edge and saw a fat white grub squirming there. With a whoop of joy he lifted other rocks and collected half a dozen of the wriggling larvae.

There was nothing that looked like a fish pole anywhere in the basin but Dick cut an eight-foot bough from one of the evergreens and trimmed it into serviceable shape. Then he set off at a trot for the lower lake where he had seen the trout jump.

A low point of rocks thrust out into the lake at one place. It seemed to offer a chance to cast in deeper water, and he made his way out to the tip of the point, watching eagerly for signs of fish. To his disappointment the surface lay like a blue mirror under the noon sun. Not a ripple marred it and even the flies appeared to have gone elsewhere.

Nevertheless he had to have a try at it. He put one of the grubs on his hook and made an experimental cast. The bait flew out forty feet or more and struck with a plop. He started trailing it slowly toward him, preparing to try again. Suddenly there was a commotion in the water and he felt a strike that jarred the rough pole almost out of his hands.

The next five minutes were packed with the wildest kind of action. Having no rod and no reel, Dick had to depend on sheer muscle, the strength of his line and the toughness of his spruce bough. Fortunately the gut leader held, and the fish was so securely hooked that it could not shake loose.

The boy gasped when he saw the size of the trout. Leaping clear of the water in a frenzied effort to free its mouth, it looked nearly two feet long. Back and forth it dashed, stirring up a foaming arc at the end of the taut line, while Dick struggled to keep his feet on the rock. At last he felt a slackening in the trout's furious rushes. It was beginning to tire. With no way to reel in line there was only one thing he could do—work his way backward along the point, hauling the fish after him.

Somehow he managed to keep the line tight, even when the trout started its final battle. He was panting and his arms shook when he jerked his prize out of water at the end. For a while he just sat there in the heather, feasting his eyes on the big fish. It was a good twenty inches in length and he was sure it weighed over four pounds.

Before he got back to camp he had raised that guess to seven or eight pounds, and a hollowness under his belt told him it was past lunchtime. He started a blaze in the stone fireplace and set about cleaning his catch for the pan. But before he used a knife on that bright beauty, he had to show it to his father.

"Yo-o-o, Dad!" he yelled through cupped hands. And when the distant figure raised its head he held the big fish up at arm's length. In a moment the little scientist had closed his specimen-box and was coming down the meadow. Dick went part way to meet him, carrying the trout.

"Great heavens!" Dr. Randolph exclaimed. "A rainbow—and a big one, at that! I thought Craig told us there were no fish in these lakes. How'd you catch him?"

Dick told the whole story while he cleaned the trout

and put slices in the skillet with sizzling bacon. There was enough of the delicious pinkish brown meat to give each of them a huge meal. For a while they sat there contentedly, discussing the surprising presence of rainbow trout in Four Lakes Basin. No theory either of them could advance seemed to fit the facts, and at the end of half an hour's talk, Dr. Randolph got up with a laugh.

"I won't be satisfied till we find a scientific explanation," said he. "But that's no reason to look a gift horse in the mouth. The fish are here, and hungry for bait. I think I'll have a try at it myself tomorrow."

He went back to his plant study while Dick washed up and tidied the camp. With most of the afternoon still ahead of him he decided to do some more exploring.

First he checked up on his marmot trap. This time he approached the colony from the meadow instead of taking the more difficult route along the outside of the rim. From half a mile away he could see the animals feeding and playing as usual on the rocky slopes. He made no effort to conceal himself, and as he drew nearer all the marmots hustled into their burrows, obeying the warning whistles of the sentinels.

Dick climbed to the spot near the top of the ridge where he had set his trap. Everything was just as he had left it. Not a grain of dirt or a blade of grass had been disturbed, as far as he could see. Whether the big marmot had simply stayed in his hole or had used some secret rear entrance, the boy had no way of telling. He searched the ledges above the burrow for several minutes and finally found a deep, narrow crevice between two rocks, with what might be a marmot hole at the bottom, under an overhanging shelf of stone. Unable to reach it with his arm, he had to content himself with dropping half a dozen good-sized rocks into the cranny. If this was the animal's back door, he thought he had it blocked.

From the top of the ridge he could look off across a jumble of peaks and ranges to the west. Rising a little above the others was the hoary head of what he thought must be Mt. Olympus. He wished there was a chance to climb it, but though it seemed to be so near he knew the big peak was at least thirty miles away.

That need not stop him from doing some mountaineering, however. Lifting steeply from the northwest wall of the basin was a snow-covered crest that had challenged him from the moment he set eyes on it. Somewhere up there among the crags he thought he might find the nest of the bald eagle he had seen that morning.

Filled with energy and ambition he pulled his belt a notch tighter and set off briskly to scale the peak.

Eight

FROM THE SOUTH SHOULDER OF THE
mountain a long, rocky hogback fell away to join the
basin rim. Dick decided his best route was along the top
of this ridge. He left the meadow below and went up a
giant staircase of ledges to the top of the rampart.

He had gone only a hundred yards up the hogback
when he found it narrowed to a knife-edge, sharp as the
ridgepole of a house. For some distance he had to move

cautiously, balancing like a tight-rope walker as he climbed. Then the ridge grew a little wider, with snow slides descending on both sides. He had to watch every step to avoid slipping on the icy rocks.

So intent was he on keeping his footing that a sudden sound ahead startled him. He looked up to find the steep shoulder of the mountain only fifty feet away. And there on a ledge, high above him, a big, shaggy, white animal was standing.

"Mountain goat!" he started to exclaim. But before his lips could frame the whisper, the beast turned nimbly, jumped to a lower shelf, trotted along it for a few yards and disappeared around a jutting cornice of rock.

Dick had had no time to get out his camera, but he was delighted nevertheless. A dozen times he had heard debates about the presence of mountain goats in the Olympics. Now he had the evidence of his own eyes. Before he left he resolved to get the proof permanently on film.

The cliff ahead of him was broken by a series of ledges, and a few moments' study showed him what looked like a way up. He started climbing and found most of the ascent easy enough. There was one place, near the top, where he had to haul himself up by his arms, depending on a scant inch of outcropping rock for a foothold. It was ticklish business but he made it on the first try and lay resting on the ledge, looking back over the basin.

At his left, close to the northern end of the ledge, a smooth crust of snow dropped away at a 45-degree angle to the flowery meadow far below. It looked inviting—a fast and easy short-cut on the way home. But he wasn't ready to return yet. Now that he had made his way this far up the peak, he meant to go still higher.

The crag around which the goat had vanished was only a few yards to his right. He picked his way along the rocky shelf, pressing his body tightly against the cliff where the ledge was narrowest. How a four-footed animal as big as the one he had seen could have moved so briskly along that six-inch strip of rock was something to marvel at.

Dick reached the turn in safety and found a broader foothold on the northwest shoulder of the cliff. Right ahead of him a rough slope led upward almost to the mountain's summit. It was steep and rocky, but it promised better climbing than anything he had encountered so far.

Up to that moment his attention had been wholly on the cliff face and the higher slopes. Now for the first time he turned his eyes to the west, and what he saw caused the breath to catch in his throat. It wasn't the mighty panorama of the peaks that made him gasp. Nearer, spread below him at the foot of a glittering slant of snow, lay an emerald-green valley with a tiny blue lake near its center. The grassy floor was hardly more than half a mile across. It lay at the bottom of a huge bowl, two thousand feet lower than the surrounding mountains. And moving very slowly along the other side of the lake were six or seven brownish dots that could only be grazing elk.

For several minutes the boy stood there watching the scene below in fascination. He pulled out his camera and shielded the lens from the afternoon sun while he took a picture. The little herd of elk was probably too far off to show up in the photograph, but he hoped he had captured some part of the valley's wild loveliness.

Glancing up at the mountain wall on the opposite side, he saw something else moving there on the cliffs. It was more than a mile away and barely visible, but he was certain its color was too dark for a mountain goat. A bear, perhaps, or a cougar? He wished fervently for a pair of good field-glasses, but without them all he could do was guess. The animal, whatever it might be, disappeared in a cleft of the rocks after a moment or two. He still stared at the spot where it had been and shook his head. Something about the moving speck had been unlike either bear or cougar. If he had trusted his eyes at that distance, he would have said the beast was walking on its hind legs.

Dick turned with regret from the hidden valley and started up the rock scarp. Tomorrow, if the weather held fair, he vowed to find a way down into that magically green meadow. Meanwhile he still had the peak to climb.

Toiling higher and higher with occasional pauses for rest, he arrived at last within a few yards of the top. There remained only a jagged twenty-foot crag to be scaled. He looked up at it, planning the safest route, and saw a shaggy white head with two black horns appear over the edge of the low cliff. The goat regarded him steadily and without any noticeable sign of fear.

Very slowly Dick opened the case at his belt and drew out the camera. He had to change the setting, for this time his subject was barely a dozen yards away. In the finder he saw the big animal's bearded face, but now it had come a step nearer the edge and most of its body was visible. He held his breath and clicked the shutter. At the sound, the goat pawed at the rocks and shook its horns threateningly.

Dick chuckled and put the camera away. But even as he fastened the flap of the case there came a scrabbling sound above. He jerked his head up in time to see the big hairy beast in the air, all four sharp black hoofs pointed directly at him. Acting on instinct, the boy threw himself sidewise. He fell against a boulder as the goat landed, a scant yard away. Apparently the animal had no intention of staying to finish him. It went bounding off down the scarp in a series of stiff-legged jumps.

"Whew!" Dick panted as he picked himself up. "That could have been curtains. I'll have to remember—never corner a mountain goat on top of a peak unless you've got a gun."

He climbed the cliff and sat for a few minutes on the pinnacle of the mountain. The sun went down behind a bank of haze over the western peaks and a cold wind began to blow. In the shadowy light the basin, the hidden valley and the soaring masses of the Olympics took on a wild, unearthly beauty.

Dick looked around for the eagle's nest but there was no sign of it. Perhaps it was built on one of the lower crags, along the inaccessible eastern side. Neither did he find any evidence that the peak had been climbed before. Quite possibly, he realized with a thrill, the great goat and he were the only living things that had ever reached this high place on foot. He picked up a sharp rock and hammered his initials and the date into the stone face of the summit.

By the time he finished it was growing late—time to start down if he meant to reach camp before dark. He made a quick descent of the rocky slope, worked his way around the corner of the lower cliff, and paused at the top of the snow slide. He had never tried a glissade on smooth crust, but it looked inviting.

He stepped out cautiously on the icy slant. For a moment the nails in his shoes held. Then both feet went out from under him and he found himself on his back, shooting down the roof-like slope at express-train speed. There was nothing he could do to slow up his progress, and the meadow was whizzing nearer every second. He braced himself for the shock. Then, miraculously, it was over. He slid out into the heather and came to a gentle stop, breathless but unhurt.

Dick got to his feet with a feeling of exhilaration. "Boy!" he murmured to himself. "No more hiking down mountains for me, when I can find one of those things!"

ACTING ON INSTINCT, THE BOY THREW HIMSELF SIDEWISE

He made the three miles up the meadow in half an hour, walking and running by turns, and arrived just at dusk. His father had already started the supper fire and was stirring the batter for flapjacks while he brushed away swarms of midges.

"Flies are bad tonight," he remarked. "We'll have to keep a smudge going till we get to sleep. Where've you been all afternoon, son?"

Dick told him about his explorations and the adventure with the goat. "If the camera's still all right," he said, "I've got a picture that ought to settle all arguments about Rocky Mountain goats in the Olympics. But the best thing I found was a valley, over on the northwest side of the rim. It must be thousands of feet lower than the basin—full of fine, green grass—and there was a herd of elk feeding. It's so shut in by mountains I don't know whether the rangers even know it's there! Tomorrow I'm going to see if I can't get down into it and find out what it's like."

Dr. Randolph flipped the frying pan dexterously and turned a pancake brown side up. "Sounds like an interesting place," he said. "Don't take chances if the climbing's bad, though. If you want to wait a few days I'll go over with you."

"It doesn't look too tough," Dick assured him. "I can make it all right, and I'll report back to you if I find any special plants you ought to see down there."

The wind was cold and damp that evening, but it did

not blow hard enough to chase away the buzzing midges. Dick piled moist heather on the coals of the fire and they sat for an hour in the drifting smoke, coughing but free of flies. It was a relief to crawl into the sleeping bags.

Tired as he was from a long day of action, Dick didn't fall asleep at once. He lay for a while in that drowsy borderland between sleep and waking, where real things are confused with things of the imagination. Again he seemed to be standing on the cliff top overlooking the lost valley. Across from him on the far mountain he could see that antlike figure crawling. But this time its outlines were distinct, as if he looked through powerful glasses. It was no four-footed animal but a caveman—shaggy, bearded, dressed in skins and trailing a crude kind of club. "Neanderthal Man," he told himself, proud of remembering the name from his schoolbooks. "Very interesting. Must make a note of that for Dr. Castleman at the Smithsonian. I don't suppose he's had a live specimen in years."

.　　.　　.

He woke in the middle of the night, all his senses taut with alarm. It was pitch dark about him. No stars shone overhead, and there was cold mist on his face. The only thing he heard was the faint drip of moisture from the evergreen boughs. He stilled his breathing and lay motionless, straining his ears to catch some other sound. Minutes passed before he heard it—the tiny clink of a displaced pebble, some distance away.

Dick got up quietly and found the flashlight. He threw its beam in a slow circle around the camp, but the light was smothered in fog. At least there was no prowling animal near enough to be seen. After a few moments he put the flash away and got back into his eiderdown. There was nothing up here in the high basin, he assured himself, that could do him and his father any harm.

Possibly because of his wakefulness during the night, the boy overslept next morning. It was the sound of Dr. Randolph's voice that roused him—a sudden exclamation of surprise and annoyance.

"What did you do with the bacon, son?" the scientist asked. "Can't seem to find the salt, either. This place must be bewitched."

Dick staggered up sleepily and peered into the tree cuddy where the supplies were kept. He rubbed his eyes and looked again. Certain it was that their flitch of bacon had disappeared, and with it the bag of salt.

"Gosh!" said the boy. "I put 'em back there yesterday. Something must have been here in the night. Did you see any tracks?"

They searched the ground in every direction for several minutes without finding anything. Luckily Dick had a small tin box of salt in the pocket of his slicker, left over from an earlier camping trip. They ate a baconless breakfast, using the salt as sparingly as possible.

"Looks as if we had light-fingered neighbors up here," said Dr. Randolph grimly. "I've been robbed by bears and porcupines, but this doesn't seem to be their kind of work. A bear would have torn the cuddy apart and waked us up. Besides, any animal that was salt-hungry would have bitten a hole in the bag and satisfied itself right on the spot. I'm beginning to think Craig's talk about no Indians ever coming above timberline is a lot of hokum."

Dick told him about waking in the night. "I decided it was just my imagination," he said. "I did think I heard a pebble rattle, but I couldn't tell where. Guess it must have been our visitor. Anyhow, I'll keep a lookout for tracks today. Are you planning to do any fishing, Dad? If we want to eat we'd better catch some fish."

His father nodded. "I'll have a trout for supper," he replied, "if it's as easy as you say. And I'll do a little looking around, myself. You go ahead over to your valley. Say—where do you suppose this came from?"

He was stooping over near the cuddy as he spoke. Dick saw him pick up a piece of worn, dirty rawhide, two or three inches long. He took his little botanical microscope from his pocket and examined the thing more closely.

"Looks like smoked elk hide," he said. "Is it anything we brought up here?"

The boy took the scrap of leather and studied it. "No," he answered at length. "I'm pretty sure it's not. I'd say it had been used to lace a shoe—or a moccasin. But it isn't cut evenly. One end's a little narrower than the other—a homemade job. Gee, Dad, I believe you're right about our bacon-stealer being an Indian. Wait till we see Craig again. He'll have a hard time laughing this one off! Maybe this is the same man that left his hand print by the spring, down below. The one with only three fingers —remember?"

"I suppose it might be," said the scientist thoughtfully. "At any rate, I don't like his company. Perhaps it would be better if you stayed close to camp today, to keep an eye on things."

Dick laughed. "You getting jumpy, Dad?" he asked. "I don't believe we'll be bothered in daylight. Besides, there's no place for the fellow to hide here in the basin. He's probably down the mountain, somewhere in the thick timber. So there's nothing to worry about. I'll come back with my scalp on!"

Nine

THE MORNING FOG WAS BEGINNING TO
break away when Dick prepared for his expedition. The
camera had suffered no injury, he was glad to find. He
strapped the case to his belt and balanced it with his
hunting knife on the other side. The lunch he took was
small enough to be carried in his pockets. It consisted of
three or four slabs of hard biscuit, a handful of raisins
and a small bar of chocolate.

As he went down the meadow he searched constantly for tracks, but the springy heather gave no clue. He could barely tell where his own feet had trodden the moment before. At the marmot rocks he paused long enough to inspect his trap. It still lay untouched at the mouth of the burrow, and the whole hillside seemed deserted. Perhaps, he thought, the colony had moved away after his intrusion. Or were the animals merely waiting for the sun to chase away the mist before they ventured out?

In either case there was no reason for him to hang around. He tiptoed down the stony slope and resumed his journey northward. The fog was drifting off above the mountains and the morning was warm and sunny by the time he reached the northwest rampart of the basin. Following the same route as the day before, he mounted the ledges and scrambled up the sharp crest of the cleaver till he reached the cliff. This time he found the ascent easier, for he knew exactly where to place his feet and grip with his hands. From the shelf above he worked his way around the corner of the cliff and looked down once more into the green and lovely bowl of his secret valley.

A grin of delight spread over the boy's face. He hadn't dreamed it. It was real—all just as he remembered—except that the nearer side was now sheltered from the sun by the eastern peak. In that light the long snow slide stretching to the valley floor was tinged with purplish shadows.

The temptation to glissade down was almost more than

he could resist, but common sense stopped him. First he had to be sure he could get back. He leaned over the cliff edge and studied the rocky declivity that flanked the snow on its northern side. It would be a tough climb, but as far as he could see there were no impassable places. He let himself down over the cliff and dropped to the next ledge.

Moving slowly and picking his route yard by yard, it took the boy the better part of an hour to make the descent. He memorized the mountainside as he went, so that he would be able to return the same way. Once or twice he paused to look out across the valley. Against the vivid green of the grass he could see the elk coming down in single file from the fringe of timber on the upper edge of the meadow. There were four cows and three calves in the little band, and they headed straight for the margin of the little lake. Evidently they had not winded him yet, for they waded into the water and drank leisurely before going back to their grazing.

Dick descended the last few hundred feet on a more gradual slope, rough with fallen boulders and rubble. A moment later he was striding knee-deep through grass and flowers. The sun came over the eastern heights and flooded the valley with warm, golden light.

Pride of discovery made the boy want to shout and sing. He knew how Magellan and Balboa must have felt. This bit of paradise, cupped among the peaks, was all his own.

He went slowly, circling to the north around the lake, so as not to disturb the feeding elk. There was no visible outlet from the pool, and no break in the mountain wall. That bit of blue water must be fed by rain and melting snow and drawn off by evaporation.

In a few more minutes Dick had reached the western side of the valley and was staring up at the dark, forbidding cliffs that rose abruptly out of the meadow. At first glance he would have said they were unclimbable. Yet he remembered that some living creature had been moving up there yesterday, and curiosity made him take a closer look. Scouting along the base of the rocks he found a spot where the grass was beaten down for a yard or two, and from it a faint, irregular trail led off in the direction of the lake.

Thrilled by this discovery, he turned to make a more searching examination of the cliff itself. Just above the trodden grass was a tiny rock shelf, angling upward to the right. Was it possible that any animal could use it as a foothold? The ledge was a bare three inches wide. Nothing much bigger than a squirrel would be able to travel along that shelf—unless it had hands.

The idea came with a shock. He had forgotten his half-dream about the caveman until that instant. With a quickened pulse, he reached up to find a grip for his fingers, planted a foot on the ledge and started to climb. Surprisingly, it was much easier than he had expected. Convenient handholds and crevices for his steel-spiked toes seemed to appear by magic, beckoning him on. Almost before he knew it he was forty feet up the cliffside and standing on a wider ledge where he could look around.

The mountain, he discovered, was no longer a vertical wall. It slanted upward at an angle of sixty or seventy degrees, crisscrossed with outcrops and shelves of rock that promised safe climbing. But what interested him most was the trace of a path angling higher along the face of the slope. He bent down to look more closely. Could he be wrong—or had those stones been rubbed smooth by other feet?

He glanced up at the sun. It was still an hour before noon, and that should give him plenty of time to reach the summit and get back. As he went upward the track he followed was lost and reappeared a dozen times. But it clung to the natural contour of the mountainside, zigzagging higher and higher in a series of switchbacks, and the boy grew surer than ever that he was on a beaten path.

It was hot work. He rested once or twice, looking down into the valley and across to the opposite rim. The elk were feeding unconcernedly in the meadow above the lake. On a high crag to the north of the snow slide he could make out a white dot that moved. His old friend the mountain goat had evidently returned, undaunted by yesterday's encounter.

He thought he must be three-quarters of the way up when the steep track suddenly swung around an outcropping boulder and he found himself looking into an enormous cleft in the rock. It was only a few yards wide and hundreds of feet deep—a chasm like an ax stroke splitting the crest of the mountain.

This must be the spot where the moving speck had vanished while he was watching it, the afternoon before. He hesitated before entering the cleft. It was dark as twilight in there, for the sun could penetrate it for only a few feet. A mass of ice and fallen debris from the cliffs above filled the bottom. And the path, if path it was, followed a rough shelf up the north wall of the chasm.

Dick drew a long breath and went in. It was many degrees colder inside. Moisture dripped from the dank rocks and the ledge on which he moved was wet and treacherous. He went slowly, half feeling his way, and more than once he was tempted to turn back. But the thrill of exploration was throbbing in his veins now. Over and over, those lines of Kipling beat like tom-toms in his head—"Something lost behind the ranges; lost and waiting for you—go!"

His hands were scratched and raw from clinging to the rocks and his knees shook with weariness when he crawled out at last on a wider shelf. It was perhaps a hundred and fifty feet above the floor of the chasm, and so far back into the mountain that he could no longer see out to the valley. How long it had taken him to reach this spot he had no way of telling.

For five minutes he was content to lie flat on his back

and rest. Then, doggedly, he got to his feet again, prepared to go on. With a feeling of dismay he discovered that the far corner of the ledge he was on marked the end of any possible climbing. The cliff wall went up smooth and straight without a visible foothold. But the path—where did it go from here? Surely no creature, animal or human, would scale those dizzy heights for the sole purpose of reaching the barren shelf of rock on which he stood.

Finally the answer came to him. Without his realizing it, the chasm had become narrower as he advanced, and opposite the end of the ledge the farther wall was a scant three feet away. He was at the entrance to a "chimney." Looking up, he could see bright daylight only a few yards above his head. A good climber with plenty of nerve might cover that distance by bracing his back and legs against the two walls.

Dick shivered a little at the idea. He had done a bit of chimney-work once, in the Adirondacks, but there the drop below him was only a few feet. Here—he closed his eyes, refusing to look down. He felt of his shoe-nails and they were still firm and sharp. It seemed obvious now that someone had gone up that way before him. He thought he could make it, but if he waited much longer he knew he would never bring himself to start.

Gritting his teeth he leaned across the crevice, braced his hands on the farther wall and eased his body around until both shoulders were planted against the rock. The distance was just wide enough to give his bent knees leverage. He raised his left foot a few inches, getting a firm hold with the spikes. One shoulder, then the other, squirmed higher as the leg straightened. Now the right foot lifted, and again he inched his back up the wall.

It was slow work, but once he got the hang of it his fear left him. He was cool enough until his upward progress had taken him within a yard of the top. Then, in panic, he began wondering whether he could get safely out of the chimney. Above him was what looked like the sharp edge of a cliff, on the side he was facing. The crag at his back went some distance higher.

Well, he told himself, there was nothing to do but keep going. If it looked impossible when he got there, he could still let himself down the way he had come.

He planted his feet, one above the other, flexed his tired leg muscles and hunched his shoulders up the rock wall. At last his boot soles were resting on the brink of a broad, snowy shelf. Taking a few seconds to gather his strength, he turned his body cautiously till his face was toward the cliff. Then, with a powerful shove of his arms he pushed himself erect and staggered back, away from the yawning abyss.

It was good to stand in daylight again and look up to a fair-sized patch of blue sky between the towering crags. He rubbed his thighs to get rid of the trembling in them. A warm glow of pride in his achievement filled him, and he decided, a trifle cockily, that he was a real mountain climber.

That puffed-up feeling lasted only a moment, however. As soon as he looked about him at the surface of the ledge, he had something more important to think about. The tracks of his nailed boots were not the only ones that showed in the half-frozen snow. A short distance beyond the place where he stood, there was the print of a moccasined foot, long and broad and unmistakable!

Dick drew a quick breath. He knew now that the climbing figure he had seen was a man. The same man, perhaps, who had stolen their salt and bacon the night before. He got down on his knees to stare at the moccasin track. What would bring a lone Indian into this high country among the forbidding peaks? It was against all the rules of Indian behavior that he had heard discussed. The man must be in hiding from the law. And in that case, how would he deal with a stranger who trespassed on his secret domain?

Slowly and with a sense of foreboding, the boy moved up along the ledge. The tracks were still there, beckoning him on, but now he followed them less eagerly. His eyes shifted from the trail to the place, a few yards ahead, where it vanished around a shoulder of the cliff. What lay beyond he could not tell. But he had a feeling it might be dangerous to find out.

Three or four more strides and he halted abruptly before a foot-wide crack in the rock at his right. A moccasin print, veering off from the path, had directed his attention to the cranny, and now he saw a scattering of red-brown spots in the snow that looked like frozen blood. He took a cautious step closer and peered into the half darkness.

The crevice, he saw, was filled with ice, packed there by winter storms. But out of it a sort of cupboard had been hollowed. The bottom of the cavity was breast-high and it extended back into the ice for several feet. And lying snugly in that natural freezing chamber was meat —a big, bloody haunch that had the appearance of an over-sized quarter of lamb.

Dick backed away quickly, his heart pounding. What he had discovered was a cache of elk venison, and it meant only one thing. He was close—too close—to the hide-out of a big-footed, moccasin-shod savage who had no scruples against illegal killing.

Ten

THE BOY MADE HIS WAY BACK TO THE TOP
of the chimney. He tried to move quietly and fast, but
he stumbled in his haste, and the crunch of his boots in
the snowy crust sounded loud as thunder in his ears.
The chasm opened below him, terrifyingly deep, but at
that moment he was far more afraid of being caught
there on the ledge than of the dangerous descent.

Hurriedly he leaned across the open space, twisted his

back against the cliff and began to let himself down. It was only after he had lowered his body a few yards that he realized what would happen if one of his feet slipped. For ten seconds he hung there, eyes shut, fighting to get a grip on himself. Then he went to work again, doggedly planting his spiked soles and sliding down, foot by foot.

At last he stood safely on the shelf below. He drew a long breath and relaxed his muscles, leaning back against the wall of the chimney. And at that instant, as he glanced upward, a scrap of rock hardly bigger than a pea fell past him from overhead. After long seconds he heard it rattle on the stones at the bottom of the cleft.

For the space of half a dozen heartbeats he stared at the patch of sky above. There was nothing there—no face peering down at him—no faintest sound. Nevertheless he had a feeling that he was in deadly peril while he stood on that ledge. Hugging the cliff wall he started down the long slant toward the outer end of the crevice.

The minutes that passed before he came out into daylight on the mountainside seemed more like hours. He was astonished, when he looked up at the sun, to find it was only a little after noon.

He scrambled down the rock-strewn slope, keeping to the path he had followed on the way up. There was only the cliff face to descend, and he dropped the last few feet into the soft meadow grass.

For some reason the valley no longer looked as romantic to him as it had that morning. He spent no time admiring its beauty, but crossed its green expanse as fast as his tired legs would carry him. It was only when he reached the steep scarp of the eastern mountain that he stopped to rest. The food he had brought in his pockets was sodden and crumbled, but he munched it hungrily as he sat there on a boulder. And all the while his eyes watched the heights across the valley.

The dry biscuit and the chocolate made him thirsty, but he had no wish to go back, even as far as the pond. With a final look at the opposite mountain, he started his long, rough climb to the rim.

.   .   .

Almost the first thing Dick saw, as he came toiling over the crest, was a small, active figure standing on the point of rocks that jutted out into the lake. It was his father, busily wielding the fish pole.

He swung down across the meadow and soon arrived within hailing distance.

"Yo, Dad," he called. "Any luck?"

The little scientist completed his cast and looked up, peering through his spectacles.

"Well—hello, son," he answered. "Back kind of early, aren't you? Look as if you'd been through a rock crusher. What happened to your clothes?"

The boy glanced down at his tattered shorts and shirt. It was the first time that day that he had spared them a thought.

"Gee!" he said ruefully. "I did give 'em some wear an' tear, didn't I? Guess I was too busy to notice. The climbing over there is plenty rugged. Dad—"

But he checked himself. He didn't want to worry his father yet. "How's the fishing?" he asked.

"Oh, so-so." Dr. Randolph was trying to speak in an offhand manner, but there was a gleam of almost boyish satisfaction in his eye as he gestured toward the bank. Still flopping there in the heather were two handsome rainbow trout.

"Swell, Dad! You're a real fisherman," Dick grinned. "They're not quite as big as mine, but mighty nice as trout go."

His father snorted and began looping up his line. "No use casting any more," he grumbled. "All your loud chatter has frightened the fish to the bottom."

Each of them took one of the trout and they started up the meadow.

"Did you bring me any botanical specimens?" asked Dr. Randolph.

"Sorry, Dad. I don't believe there was anything unusual, though. Some larkspur and Indian paint-brush—and the grass the elk feed on. I meant to pick some on my way back. Forgot, I guess."

"Yes," said his father. "I was up there at the head of the snow slide when you started across the valley. It looked to me as if you were in quite a hurry."

"You were watching me? Say—did you—I mean, what

did you think of the valley?"

"One of the loveliest places in America, I'm sure," the scientist replied soberly. "Or in any other country, for that matter. You may as well tell me, Dick. What were you running away from?"

The boy flushed a little under his tan. "Well, Dad, I'll admit I was scared. Maybe you won't blame me, though, when I tell you the whole story."

He began at the beginning and gave an account of all that had happened.

"When I saw that haunch of elk meat," he said, "I decided to get out of there in a hurry. It was queer, too, about that little chunk of rock that fell, just as I got out of the chimney. Maybe he was up there, watching me. It gave me cold chills to think how easy it would have been to knock me off right then. You'd probably have found what was left of me down at the bottom after a couple of days, and there wouldn't be a thing to show I hadn't just slipped and fallen.

"I didn't want to give him any more chances like that, so I came away fast."

"Yes," smiled Dr. Randolph. "I see what you mean. Under the circumstances I should probably have acted the same way. But looking at it from a detached viewpoint, I doubt if you were in any great danger. Remember, this fellow is just a sneak thief. Probably some poor Indian that's gone to seed—wanted for chicken-stealing or some kind of petty larceny. So he comes up here where nobody's likely to look for him, does a little poaching to keep alive, and when he's hungry for salt he waits till we're asleep and raids our provisions. Does that sound very desperate?"

Dick was feeling small. He couldn't deny the logic of his father's reasoning.

"All right," he laughed sheepishly. "So I've got too much imagination. I was running away from a shadow. But I'll say this for your Indian—he must have squirrel blood. Anybody who can go up that chimney with moccasins on is no slouch of a climber!"

It was still several hours before sunset when they reached the camping place. Dr. Randolph took his specimen-boxes and went out across the meadow to continue his botanizing. Dick got a needle and thread out of his kit and did some rough and ready mending on the rents in his clothes.

While he was at work he remembered with a twinge of conscience that he had been neglecting the real business of his trip. He had learned very little about silver marmots and had made no progress whatever at catching them.

There was time before supper to go down the meadow and do some observing. He made his way cautiously along the rim, so as to approach the marmot castle from the rear once more.

Lying flat on his stomach he could command a good view of the rocks below. Ten or twelve of the animals were in sight, but this time only the larger ones seemed to be out. The playful pups must already have been packed off to bed in their snug nests, deep in the hillside. From that point Dick could not see the entrance of the old sentinel's burrow, and he looked in vain for the big marmot among those that were feeding farther down the slope.

For the next twenty minutes he lay watching their movements. One of their favorite foods seemed to be the roots of little mountain lilies that grew in the lower crevices. They would dig expertly with their forepaws, unearth the tuber and strip off its outer skin. Then, sitting up like overgrown squirrels, they would munch each tidbit solemnly. Others nibbled at the stems of tiny cloverlike plants among the heather at the edge of the meadow. It was all so peaceful that he almost hated the mission that had brought him here. However, he told himself sternly, the interests of science would not be served unless he took back the skins of a couple of silver marmots.

After a while he got unwillingly to his feet and watched the alarmed animals race for their holes. A few steps took him down to the burrow where he had set his trap. At first he thought it was still as he had left it. Then he took another startled look. The clog was across the entrance to the hole and the chain ran out of sight inside. His fingers moved toward the clog, then drew back. He remembered in time that if he hauled the trapped marmot out he was likely to have a battle on his hands.

Excited by his find, he ran all the way back to camp and got himself a club. With the solid, two-foot length of spruce in his fist, he made the return trip as quickly as possible and arrived breathless at the burrow once more. Warily he took hold of the clog, prepared to put all his weight into the pull. At the first heave he nearly fell over backward. The chain and the sprung trap came whisking out of the hole, but there was no marmot. Instead, all he found in the tight jaws was a trio of long-clawed toes, cleanly bitten off just above the steel.

Dick was more than disappointed. As he stood there holding the trap in his hands, it seemed to him that the whole expedition was a failure. He could picture himself going back to Washington and telling Dr. Castleman he had fallen down on his assignment. Even if the color photos turned out well they would be of little use without mounted animals for the exhibit.

He took the trap over to the lake, washed it well and reset it. Then he returned to the marmot colony and concealed it as before, in the opening of another burrow farther down the hill. It was a faint hope, but for the moment it was the best he could do. Tired and discouraged, he picked up his club and went slowly up the meadow toward camp.

When he had cleaned the trout and started the supper fire, he had cause to remember again their thieving visitor of the night before. Without bacon grease it would be a messy job trying to fry the fish in the pan. Finally he hit on the idea of running a long green stick through them and broiling them over the coals. It was a slow process. One of the fish persisted in falling into the fire, and he had to haul it out several times, its skin and outer flesh charred and black with ashes.

Fortunately Dr. Randolph wasn't fussy about food. He ate the trout without complaining and Dick found it tasted better than it looked.

While they were washing up after the meal he told his father about the marmot trap.

"Well, you had him for a little while, at least," said the scientist. "That shows you had the trap set right. Maybe next time you'll have better luck."

"Yes, but our time's nearly half gone," Dick answered. "It'll be a week tomorrow since we left the Ranger camp."

He yawned wearily, and his father peered at him through the smudge smoke.

"You'd better turn in, son," he counseled. "You'll feel better after a night's rest. I'll sit up awhile and watch. Don't want that fellow coming back here and stealing the ax, or some of our other things. We'd really be in a pickle if he did."

"Okay, Dad." Dick yawned again. "Wake me up when you're ready for bed and I'll stand the next watch."

It was long past midnight when the boy struggled back to consciousness. His father was shaking him gently by the shoulder.

"I'm going to get a little sleep now," Dr. Randolph murmured. "Sorry to wake you, but you'll have only two or three hours before it's daylight. Keep the fire up. I thought I heard something moving out there a bit ago. Could have been wrong, but we may as well be on the safe side."

Dick threw two or three sticks on the fire and moved about to stir up his circulation. He stowed his camera and box of film, the ax and a few other valuables inside his sleeping bag and sat on its open end. At that moment he was not at all sure he could keep awake, and he wanted to be sure all their possessions would be safe.

It was cold, even within a few feet of the fire. The stars twinkled frostily overhead. Dick pulled a sweater around him and hunched his shoulders against the chill. He listened intently for several minutes but there was no sound to break the stillness.

He got to thinking about marmots and traps. Would it be worth while trying to bait the pan with food? He pictured a lily root resting temptingly between the open jaws and shook his head. Only meat-eating animals could be caught that way, he was sure.

No, there must be some other method. He considered the possibility of hiding in the rocks and rushing out with the club on the chance of catching a marmot out of reach of its burrow. Pretty crude, he thought. Even an intelligent ten-year-old ought to be able to come up with something cleverer than that.

It was about then that he remembered the fish line. Tough and strong, that line was. Perhaps it would hold a marmot—not a husky brute like the old sentinel, but an ordinary-sized one. He tried to remember, from stories he had read, how a rabbit snare was fashioned. But that, he thought, required a springy sapling growing beside the rabbit's path. There was nothing of the kind on the rocky hill where the marmots lived.

He wondered if the pole he had made would be long enough to reach from one of the holes to a place where he could lie hidden. If so, he might be able to rig a noose of line on the end of it and wait till one of the rodents stuck its head out.

Stiffly he got up and brought the pole to the fire. By the flickering light he began tying a strong loop near the end. He made it half an inch in diameter—big enough so that the running end of the noose could pass through it easily. With the end of the line in his hand he found he could jerk the noose tight in a split second.

After that he must have dosed a little, because the sky was beginning to grow lighter when next he looked about him. Off near the basin's rim a marmot whistled sharply.

Dick pursed his lips and imitated the sound. The result surprised him. His whistle came out loud and clear, and almost instantly it was answered by a dozen others, up and down the meadow.

The boy stood up, pleased with his success. He tried

it again and again, perfecting his technique. "Hot dig-
gety!" he told himself with a grin of delight. "That
whistle sure fools the marmots. It almost fools me!
Maybe I've got something there!"

Eleven

REMEMBERING THAT HIS FATHER HAD
been on watch most of the night, Dick did not wake
him for breakfast. He got a sketchy meal for himself,
made sure that none of their belongings had been disturbed, and set off for the marmot rocks.

In one hand he carried his club and in the other the
fishing pole, now equipped with its loop of line. Once
more he took the precaution of crossing the rim and ap-

proaching his hunting ground from the rear. If his new plan was to have any success he knew he should be careful to disturb the marmots as little as possible.

From his old observation post on the crest he studied the familiar jumble of rocks for some time. He wanted to fix a picture of the whole layout in his mind so that he would know the location of each hole.

There were several of the furry inhabitants sunning themselves on the ledges. The big gray marmot he had tried to trap was out of sight—probably still nursing a sore paw in his burrow.

Dick hesitated a moment before making an experiment. Now that he was so close to the animals he was less confident that his whistle would deceive them. At last he drew a deep breath, pursed his lips and tried it. The sound, perhaps because of his nervousness, was thin and unnatural. Oddly enough it did not seem to alarm the marmots. One or two looked about inquiringly, as if they wondered which one of their neighbors was such a feeble whistler, but none of them dashed for safety.

The boy grinned and went silently around to the north, keeping himself hidden behind the rocks. He had spotted a hole close to the crest, where he thought he might be able to lie concealed. In order to move more quietly he took off his shoes and put them under an overhanging ledge. Then he crept into a narrow opening between the rocks and made another survey.

The burrow he had chosen was only two or three yards

away. Very slowly he pushed the pole toward it. With a slight jerking motion he opened up the loop of fish line and let it fall around the entrance to the hole. He lay on his stomach with the butt of the spruce limb in his left hand, the free end of the cord in his right.

Now, he thought, was the time. He steadied himself, breathing evenly and prepared to whistle again. It came clear as a bell—high-pitched and piercing. As if it had been a signal, marmots answered from far and near. And almost at the same moment a brown head popped out of the burrow in front of him. For a couple of heartbeats Dick was too surprised to move. Then he pulled hard on the line. The noose slipped tight around the marmot's neck and things began to happen fast.

The sturdy animal made a frantic effort to duck back into its hole, but the tough cord held. Dick scrambled to his feet, gripping the line and the thrashing pole together in one hand while he tried to pick up his club with the other. At last he had it. Putting forth all his strength he dragged the struggling marmot out into the open, planted one foot on the pole to keep it pinned down, and aimed a solid blow at the base of the poor beast's skull.

The club fell true to the mark. In a matter of seconds the marmot's chunky body stopped quivering and it lay dead at his feet. The wild sense of triumph that had filled the boy turned to regret as he looked down at the still bundle of silvery fur. He felt like a murderer.

Below him, the slope was deserted now. Terrified by

the sudden attack, the whole colony had gone into hiding. Dick went back for his shoes and put them on. It was by the merest chance that his eye fell on the burrow where he had set his trap the second time. The clog had been moved! It was firmly wedged at the mouth of the hole.

Slowly, hating what he had to do, the boy went down the hill and grasped the clog with both hands. This time it did not come away easily. He tugged with all his might on the taut chain. And inch by inch he hauled the resisting captive out of its snug den. When its head appeared, the marmot was growling and spitting like an enraged cat. It made a lunge for his ankle, but he held it away by the chain and finished it with a quick and merciful blow of the club. Then he sat down and mopped his forehead, glad that it was over.

Two marmots in five minutes! They were all he needed to complete his mission, and now he could leave the frightened animals in peace. He was no longer sure that he wanted to be a scientist. Perhaps he wasn't cold-blooded enough. There was something wrong about killing such playful, harmless fellow-beings, even for the sake of displaying their mounted bodies in a museum collection.

He had a heavy load, going back to camp. The two marmots, though not very large, weighed about fifteen pounds apiece, and in addition he carried the trap and the fish pole. He had been glad to leave the club behind. If he never saw it again that would be all right with him.

Dick's father showed him how to skin the specimens before their bodies stiffened. He split out a pair of rough slats from the dead spruce. Then, making a crosswise incision with the hunting knife between the hind legs of one of the marmots, he began pulling the skin downward, over the body and onto the board.

There was a great deal of fat clinging to the inside of the pelts, and Dick spent the next hour scraping them clean with the blade of the knife. After that Dr. Randolph treated the raw hides with a preservative he had brought in his kit.

"They'll keep till we get down the mountain," he told the boy. "When we're back in Seattle, I'll give them another going-over before we ship them to Washington. Well, son, you've finished your assignment. What do you plan to do the rest of the time?"

Dick had been giving the matter some thought. "Of course," he said, "I'd like to help you with your collecting, if there's anything a novice like me can do. But first"—he hesitated—"I'd sort of like to explore that valley again. We ought to give Craig a complete report on the fellow who's been killing elk over there. It's a pretty serious offense, and the rangers will want to catch him in a hurry. I want to find where his camp is if I can."

Dr. Randolph gave him a long look. "You're sure you want to go?" he said. "You're not afraid?"

"That's one of the things I'd like to prove to myself," the boy grinned.

His father nodded. "Good," he said. "I don't think there's any real danger from that type of man, but it won't do any harm to be careful. I'm glad you feel that way, son."

 .   .   .

The morning had been cloudy. Now, as they finished their noon meal, a bank of fog rolled up over the rim and shrouded the basin under a moist gray blanket.

Dick knew he would take no pictures that afternoon, so he removed the camera case from his belt and put it in his bedroll for safekeeping. It would be easier climbing without that extra burden.

"See you at suppertime," he called to his father. "Don't worry about me. This fog is a help, because I can go where I want without being seen."

Three-quarters of an hour later he had reached the northwest corner of the basin and scaled the high ledge that gave access to the hidden valley. At his feet the snow slide slanted downward, its bottom lost in the gray murk.

He edged his way out on the smooth crust and in another moment he was flying down the slope at a speed that took his breath away. Around him was only the blur of fog. There were no landmarks—no way to tell how far he had come. It was uncanny to be rushing through ghostly space, on and on, powerless to stop.

As he neared the foot of the slope the darker surface of the valley floor appeared dimly through the mist. Softer snow slowed his progress. Then, before he knew it, he was catapulted into a wet, swampy spot in the level grass. He was drenched to the skin when he picked himself up, but no other damage had been done.

He thrashed his arms and ran to keep from getting chilled. By the time he reached the other side of the valley he was reasonably comfortable once more. A few moments' searching along the base of the cliff brought him to the place where he had started his earlier climb. It was not quite as easy as it had been on the first attempt. The rocks were dripping with moisture and slippery in spots, but knowing the way was a help. He went up carefully and methodically, testing the handholds to be sure he had a firm grip.

Once on the ledge, above, he was able to move faster. The trail was barely discernible in the fog, but he remembered the route well enough to follow its snakelike windings up the mountainside.

At the entrance to the cleft he paused to breathe and get his bearings. Inside that deep, narrow chasm it had been dark enough, even with the sun shining. Now its blackness was forbidding. He climbed a few steps along the ledge and waited until his eyes could adjust themselves to the gloom. Gradually he was able to make out the dim shape of the rock wall and the rugged shelf on which he stood. He went on, groping like a blind man, and after a long time he reached the last ledge at the foot of the chimney.

The wet walls looked treacherous, but he thought his

spikes would grip if he chose his footholds with care. In any case, he wasn't going to draw back now.

Once, when he was half-way up, his foot slipped and it was only by luck that the other boot sole found a firm anchorage before he fell. The experience left him weak with fright but it taught him greater caution. When he started upward again he tested each hold before putting his full weight on it. And so at last he gained the top.

The first thing he saw, when he stood on the snow-covered shelf above, was his own boot tracks, with the clear imprint of the triconi nails. The second thing he noticed was that some of those tracks were blurred over by others—the more recent prints of moccasins. That meant that the man whose hiding place he was seeking had been on the ledge after he had left it, and must now be fully aware that his trail had been followed.

The boy stood still, waiting and listening. The fog that veiled the peak was as thick as ever, and the only sound he could hear was the slow drip of moisture off the rocks. Somewhere ahead of him, in the gray cloak of mist, was the place where the ledge angled around a shoulder of the cliff. He had the eerie feeling that beyond that unseen corner someone else might be waiting and listening.

He drew his hunting knife out of its sheath and felt the comforting weight of the hilt in his hand. Then he put it back, a little ashamed. His imagination was getting the better of him again. If he had real courage, he thought, such ideas would never make him hesitate. With a kind of recklessness he moved straight on along the shelf, walked past the crevice where the elk meat was cached, and came to the jutting angle of the crag.

Involuntarily his muscles tensed as he took another slow step forward. Then, with terrible suddenness, a huge, blurred shape came at him out of the fog. He had an instant's glimpse of a bearded, glaring face—of two arms uplifted and a club swinging through the air. There was a crash—a bruising pain in his head and shoulder—and he was sprawled, face down, on the snowy ledge.

He was still partly conscious, for he had ducked in time to avoid the full impact of the blow. But try as he would, he could not seem to make his muscles do his bidding.

Powerful hands caught him by the shoulders and flung him over on his back. He felt the bite of a cord of some kind, twisted roughly around his ankles, and a moment later his wrists were bound in the same fashion. Through a haze of pain he stared up at the nightmare figure standing over him.

What he saw brought a gasp of terror from the boy's throat. This was no Indian but a creature out of the prehistoric past—a gigantic man-beast with a mat of shaggy hair and a great reddish beard. The upper body was wrapped in the skins of animals. The face and the naked, hairy arms and legs were weather-burned to a dirty shade of tan. And from under bushy brows a pair of small, fierce eyes glittered cruelly.

Dick made an effort to speak. "What—who—are you?" he asked huskily.

The man's teeth were bared for an instant in something between a grin and a snarl. But the only answer he made was a guttural grunt.

He stooped quickly, picked the boy up like a sack of meal, and flung him over his right shoulder. The skins he wore and the thick-chested body beneath them reeked of stale sweat. Still dazed from the blow, Dick felt a wave of nausea as he was jolted along. His head hung down over the man's back and he could tell little about where they were going except that the trail led downhill.

He thought his captor had taken no more than a hundred strides when the pale, misty daylight changed abruptly to darkness. They had entered a cavern of some kind, where the shuffle of moccasined feet gave back whispering echoes from the walls. Now the hairy giant stopped. He heaved Dick off his shoulder and flung him down on the stone floor.

That was the last thing the boy remembered before his mind blacked out in a swirl of dizziness and pain.

Twelve

DICK WOKE UP COUGHING, HALF STRAN-
gled by smoke. Somewhere near him a fire was flickering. Its reddish light danced eerily on the dark walls
of the cave. The boy knew where he was, but the throbbing ache in his head made it difficult to think clearly.
He lay there blinking, his eyes smarting in the smoke,
and wondered how much of what he remembered was
dream and how much reality.

After a while he tried to sit up. His hands and feet were still bound with rawhide thongs, but he managed to lift himself on one elbow. It was a relief to find his shoulder was not broken.

Three or four yards away, the bearded man was hunkered down beside the fire, holding a long strip of meat over the flames on a green stick. It gave off an appetizing smell that made Dick realize he was hungry.

The man glanced toward him, saw that he had recovered consciousness, and motioned toward a crude kind of bowl that rested on the stone floor close to Dick's feet. It was filled with water.

Gratefully he squirmed nearer and bent his head till he could get his mouth into the water. He gulped a few swallows thirstily. Then he gave a second look at the utensil out of which he had been drinking. It was made from a sheet of aluminum alloy, roughly beaten into shape with some tool like a stone hammer.

Dick's mind, still hazy, tried to grapple with the idea of a piece of modern metal in such a setting and came up against a blank wall. He felt dizzy again. Was he living in the year 10,000 B.C. or was it really the middle of the twentieth century?

While he was still groping for a clue to his situation, the shaggy figure by the fire stood up and came toward him. Instinctively Dick cowered away, but this time his captor had no hostile intent. He untied the thong that bound the boy's wrists and brought him a piece of the sizzling meat.

Dick juggled it for a moment, trying not to burn his fingers, then took a cautious nibble. It tasted good—a little like beef, but with some of the gamy flavor of venison. He wondered if it had been cut from the frozen haunch he had found in the ice crevice.

The man had returned to the fire, paying no further attention to his prisoner. Now he was wolfing down a big chunk of the hot meat, with grease dripping from his fingers. Dick's eyes rested on those huge, hairy paws and something clicked in his brain. The forefinger of the left hand was gone at the joint!

Once before, then, he had been close to this fantastic character. It seemed far more than a week ago that he had discovered the print of a big, maimed hand in the mud beside the spring. He remembered Craig's puzzled face when he saw that mark, and he wondered what the ranger would say if he knew what kind of creature had made it.

The boy lay down again. The ache in his head was less painful now but he was tired and confused. He wanted to rest and get his strength back in case he should need it.

Lying there, he wondered how long he had been in the cave. It had been early afternoon—three o'clock or before —when he reached the top of the chimney. Now it must be evening of the same day. He didn't believe he had lain unconscious for more than a few hours. His father, back in Four Lakes Basin, would be seriously worried by this time. Perhaps he was starting out with the flashlight to search for him. The boy writhed with anguish as he pictured the little scientist climbing those wicked rocks in the darkness. It was more than he could bear.

Struggling to a sitting position once more, he spoke to the man by the fire.

"What are you going to do with me?" he asked in desperation. "If you can understand, say something! I'm helpless and unarmed. I've got nothing against you. Why don't you let me go?"

The hairy face that turned toward him gave no sign of comprehension, and the only reply was another meaningless grunt. The man lifted himself erect. He stepped nearer and seized Dick's wrists. This time he twisted them behind him before binding them again with the elkskin thong. With a threatening gesture he pushed his prisoner down till he lay flat on his side. After that he gave a great yawn, stretched his massive arms and lay down beside the embers of the fire. In two or three minutes his heavy breathing told Dick he was asleep.

The boy waited till he was sure. Then he set to work doggedly to loosen his bonds. The knots, he found, were firm and cleverly tied, and the more he tugged and strained, the deeper the rawhide cut into his skin. When he gave it up at last, he was so exhausted that he fell asleep in spite of himself.

The next time he opened his eyes there was gray light

filtering into the cavern. A fragrance of broiling bacon wafted past his nose, and by craning his neck he could see that shaggy brute out of the Stone Age crouching in front of the fire again. In the man's hand was another of those heavy sheets of aluminum. He was using it as a skillet, and a number of roughly sliced rashers of bacon were crisping and curling on its surface. It took no great powers of reasoning to figure out where the savory meat had come from.

The caveman must have heard Dick stirring. He set the improvised frying pan aside and came over to the boy. The sight of his wrists, chafed and raw, seemed to strike the giant as amusing. He untied the thong, then stood up with a rumbling laugh.

"I suppose it's funny," Dick raged. "You didn't think I was going to lie here all night without trying, did you?"

It did him good to talk, and if his jailer couldn't understand the words, so much the better. The red-bearded man scowled at him a moment as if trying to interpret the noises that came from his mouth. Then he turned away, picked up two or three pieces of bacon and tossed them carelessly in Dick's lap.

The boy ate them hungrily and drank again from the water bowl. A few minutes passed while the cave dweller finished his own meal. He rose and returned to Dick. First he took the strip of rawhide and tied his hands in front of him. That done he loosened the thong at his ankles so that it made a sort of hobble, allowing him to take short steps. Finally he hauled the boy to his feet and gave him a shove toward the cave entrance. Evidently he wanted him to go outside for exercise.

Dick's joints felt stiff but he had recovered enough strength to walk without trouble. Nevertheless he thought it might be a good idea to make his captor think he was in worse shape than he actually was. Tottering feebly, he made his way to the mouth of the cavern where he stumbled and sat down, panting with apparent weakness.

The shaggy man gave that deep, scornful laugh again and turned back to his housekeeping. He seemed to regard his prisoner as safe enough.

Dick found that the cave opened on a huge shelf of rock, half a dozen yards wide and three or four times as long. At its farther edge was a precipice, dropping away almost perpendicularly into a dark, deep canyon. On the right, the ledge was effectively blocked off by a cliff. The only possible avenue of escape must be along the narrow track down which the boy had been carried after his capture.

Once he had found out the lay of the land, Dick went around to the far side of the shelf, where he was out of sight of the cavern. He made another futile effort to untie the bonds on his wrists, then gave it up and walked back and forth, giving his muscles a workout.

He had already noticed that his sheath knife was gone from his belt. Naturally that would have been the first thing a primitive human would want. Probably his shoes would be gone, too, if they had been a few sizes bigger, but nothing else on his person was worth the caveman's notice.

After twenty minutes or so he saw his jailer beckoning to him and he went obediently back to the cave mouth. The hulking red-beard seemed to be in a hurry. He snatched the thong off Dick's wrists and rebound his hands behind him. His ankles were left as they were. From a dark corner of the cave, the man picked up a huge bow of cedar wood, strung with elk sinew, and a rawhide quiver that held half a dozen feathered arrows. Then, with a threatening wave of his fist, he motioned to the boy to get back into the cave. In another moment he was gone, his feet padding swiftly up the path.

Dick felt a sudden surge of hope. Here might be his chance to escape! He stole to the entrance and stood there, listening. The caveman was already beyond earshot, doubtless making his way down the chimney to hunt in the valley. But what was he hunting? There was enough meat in the ice crevice to last a week. A cold fear shook the boy as he thought of his father.

Perhaps he could build a fire outside on the ledge, and send up a smoke signal the scientist would see. But no—anything like that might lure him straight into danger.

In a kind of frenzy, Dick rushed back into the cave. He was searching for something sharp—something he could use to saw through the thong that held his wrists.

He knelt beside the aluminum skillet and examined its edges. They had been beaten smooth with some heavy implement. He was about to move on when he noticed that one side of the heavy metal sheet showed irregular blisters and a rough, crystallized surface wholly different from the rest. It had been burned—heated to the melting point. No little cooking fire could have done that to a piece of aluminum-steel alloy a full eighth of an inch thick.

A picture flashed through Dick's mind—the fierce blaze of a crashed airplane. He had seen it happen once, back in Washington. That metal lying at his feet had once been part of a wing or a fuselage. But how had it come into the caveman's possession?

He hurried to the darker part of the cave to look at the water container again. It must have taken days of work with a rock hammer to give the thing its basin shape. But down on one side he could see a battered remnant of black paint that he thought must once have been part of a letter or number.

Hot on the trail now, he made a more careful survey of the cavern. The first discovery he made was startling enough. High on a narrow ledge of rock, where last night's firelight had failed to strike, sat three grinning human skulls. They were blackened with smoke but complete, even to the teeth. And in the jaw of one he could see the faint glitter of a gold filling.

The next thing he noticed was a heavy goatskin robe

135

hanging on a peg driven into a crack in the stone. Half hidden behind it, a pair of hand-hewn skis leaned against the wall.

Finally he went to the corner where the caveman's bow had stood. Rummaging with his toe in a heap of dust and rubble he unearthed a broken arrow with the head still on it. As he had half expected, the point was another bit of aluminum, hammered out and roughly sharpened by whetting on a stone. That might be the implement he needed. Starting to kick it out on the cave floor where he could get at 'it, he uncovered something else. It was a rumpled piece of canvas that looked like part of a parachute pack. And stenciled on it in dim but unmistakable letters were the words "U. S. NAVY."

The whole scene became shockingly clear as he stood staring at the tattered cloth. He could imagine the Navy plane with its crew of three—a TBF Avenger, perhaps —roaring in through the fog on its way to Whidbey or Sand Point. Then the tearing crash as it struck a hidden peak—the burst of flame when the high octane gas caught fire—and the final, lonely silence when the shattered plane had tumbled into some snow-filled gulch below.

It would never have been found. Searching aircraft, flying low above the crowded peaks, might cruise back and forth for weeks without sighting the buried wreckage. But when the spring thaws came the prowling caveman must have discovered it. The skulls, the 'chute-pack and the scraps of aluminum told their own grim story.

Dick's knees were shaking as he squatted, hands behind him, trying to pick up the broken arrowhead. Up to that time he had not admitted to himself how scared he was. Now he knew he had to get away quickly. If he stayed here much longer he would either be killed by the sub-human creature that held him prisoner—or lose what was left of his sanity.

With the arrow clutched in his fingers he crawled to his sleeping place at the rear of the cave and sat down. The three or four inches of shaft that remained attached to the point gave him something to hold onto while he hacked away clumsily at the thong.

Fortunately for him he had made no real progress at cutting the rawhide, for a moment or two later the red-bearded giant came back to the cave. There was barely time to slip the arrowhead into the right-hand pocket of his shorts.

If the caveman had been hunting, he returned empty-handed. Flinging down his bow and quiver in the corner, he came stalking toward the boy, a scowl of displeasure on his ugly face. He jerked Dick to his feet and made a quick inspection of the thong that bound his wrists. Apparently satisfied, he gave him a push that sent him toppling to the ground again and went to the cave mouth, where he sat staring moodily out at the peaks, now shrouded in mist.

Dick lay on his side and tried to rest. He didn't dare work on the thong again while the man was there. If he were caught at it he would lose the precious bit of aluminum that might be his one hope.

After a long time the man got up. He poked the water basin with his foot, saw it was nearly empty, and took it outside with him. In four or five minutes he brought it back full. There must be a spring or a runnel of snow water somewhere close by.

Next he went into the darkness, far at the back of the cavern, and reappeared with a crude bark basket, half filled with dried blueberries. He sat munching them by the handful but made no move to offer any to Dick.

When he had satisfied his taste for fruit, he brought some chunks of elk meat from the snow cache. The fire had burned itself out. He rebuilt it, lighting the tinder with a spark he struck from a bit of flint with his knife blade.

Dick watched these preparations with interest. His breakfast had been too scanty to give him much nourishment, and the smell of the broiling meat made him ravenous.

It wasn't until the caveman had gorged himself that he paid any attention to his prisoner. At last he slouched across the floor and went through the routine of unbinding the boy's wrists and tying them again in front of him. With a careless motion he threw him what was left of the meat.

Dick was finishing the final morsel and licking his fingers when he saw the gorilla-like figure by the fire move suddenly. The man sprang up and went with stealthy tread to the cave entrance. He stood there listening for several seconds. Then he turned in obvious alarm —stamped out the fire—flung the contents of the water bowl over the coals. Moving fast, he jerked the goatskin off the wall and swept his belongings into it, making a heavy bundle that he gripped under one huge arm.

"Come on, you," he snarled, and seizing Dick by the shoulder he hurried him back into the depths of the cave.

Thirteen

WHILE HE WAS BEING HUSTLED THROUGH
the darkness, his feet stumbling on the uneven rock,
Dick's stunned mind tried to adjust itself. The ruffian
who was dragging him along had spoken three words
in a kind of guttural English. He had heard him plainly.
Something really upsetting must have happened to make
the man drop his Stone-Age pose. Did it mean help
was coming?

He tried to pull away, but the powerful hand that gripped his arm was ruthless. They were in a narrow, pitch-black passage now, scrambling upward over rough ledges. In places the roof of the hole was so low that they had to crouch almost double. Then a glimmer of light came around a bend in the passage, and in a moment they crawled out on a wide shelf of rock, open to the gray, foggy sky.

Dick had no time to look around. His captor pulled him to the left and began climbing among a maze of crags and boulders. There was no visible path but the giant seemed to know where he was going. Once or twice he paused to listen, then hurried on again, hauling the boy after him up the rugged ledges.

At last, when Dick was beginning to wonder if he could take another step, the caveman snatched him into a crevice that was barely two feet wide. It zigzagged twice, then widened out beneath an overhanging rock that formed a shallow cavern, completely hidden from outside.

This was the end of their journey. Bruised and battered, Dick was allowed to slump down on the ledge, where he lay panting, too tired even to think.

It was several minutes before he was able to look around him and take stock of the situation. When he sat up he saw the bearded man crouching a few yards away. His attitude was still tense as he stared into the blanket of fog, listening to catch some expected sound.

This hideaway had evidently been used before. There

was a heap of blackened ashes on the ledge. The place could hardly be called a cave, for it extended only a dozen feet back under the wide canopy of rock. While it would make a poor permanent home, it afforded some shelter from the weather, and its greatest advantage was the fact that it was so well concealed.

Dick thought they must have climbed at least half a mile to reach it. Anyone trying to follow them might wander for days in that labyrinth of broken rock without finding the place, even in clear weather.

As the afternoon dragged by, the big cave dweller seemed more at ease. Whatever had been worrying him was no longer to be feared. He stretched his hairy arms, walked about a little, and gnawed on some scraps of dried meat which he took from the goatskin bundle. Once he looked at Dick with that terrifying, wolfish grin, but he said nothing. The boy began to wonder whether he had actually spoken, down there in the cave. But he couldn't be mistaken. His memory of that moment was too vivid.

When it began to grow dark the bearded man bound Dick's ankles tightly and tied his wrists behind him once more. For one frightened moment the boy thought his captor had noticed the bulge of the arrowhead in his tattered shorts, but he went away without discovering it. There was no fire that night—no food and no water. Hungry, thirsty and cold, Dick lay shivering until the caveman had stretched himself out on the ledge and begun to snore. Then, twisting his arms almost out of their sockets, he succeeded in getting the broken arrow from his side pocket.

The boy worked his body into a sitting position and set to work noiselessly on the rawhide that held his wrists. It was awkward and tiring, and he could only guess whether the thong was starting to fray. But he kept at it with dogged desperation. Weak as he was, he had a feeling he would never escape unless he succeeded now, before it was too late.

Once he dropped the arrowhead with a clatter that sounded disastrously loud in the silence, but the burly figure at the cavern entrance only stirred uneasily and continued snoring. After a long time Dick felt a strand of the elkhide thong give suddenly. It parted and fell away and his hands were free!

He rested for a few breaths, then tackled the bonds at his ankles. They proved much easier, for as soon as the numbness was out of his fingers he could tell by touch what progress he was making.

While he worked, his mind was racing ahead, trying to plan the next step. There was no club or other weapon at hand except the big cedar bow and Dick's own hunting knife. And both of them were snugly tied up in the bundle that was serving the caveman as a pillow. He considered for a wild moment the idea of searching for a rock big enough to brain his jailer, but somehow he knew he could never do such a thing in cold blood. What he wanted most was to put all possible distance between himself and the sleeping man.

The thongs were off his ankles now. With trembling fingers he untied his nailed boots and removed them, holding them in one hand. Very cautiously he got to his feet. For long seconds he listened to the heavy breathing of the bearded caveman. Then he tiptoed around him out into the fog.

As he went forward through the inky darkness, Dick knew the terror a blind person would feel, alone and in unfamiliar surroundings. The first few steps were fairly easy. He made his way through the twisting passage between walls of rock that were cold and clammy to the touch. It was when he came out on the steep ledges that he began to be afraid. There had been small chance to notice landmarks while he was being dragged up that tortuous ascent. For all he knew there might be a precipice close by—empty space yawning before his feet.

He stood still, fighting back his fear, concentrating with all his might on remembering the climb. Whatever happened he was determined to keep going. In spite of all the confusion of boulders and crags through which they had threaded their way, he believed the whole slope funneled down to one small area at its foot—the rocky ledge above the cave's rear entrance.

With this conviction firmly in his mind, the boy started down the mountainside. He still carried his shoes, but his sock-clad feet held well on the bare wet stone. He stepped carefully, trying to avoid the scraps of broken rock that hurt when he trod on them. His hands were always out in front of him, feeling for unseen obstacles.

Soon he found that other senses were replacing his eyes. Once, when he was two or three yards away from a cliff that barred his way, he knew it was there from a difference in the sound of his breathing, reflected back off the face of the stone. Again, a cold updraft of air on his legs warned him of a break in the ledge ahead. It was a drop of only a few feet, but he could easily have broken an arm or a leg if he had fallen from the top.

Dick had no idea of the passage of time. He only knew he had been moving slowly downward—groping, sliding, stumbling, through what seemed like endless hours— when he felt level ground under his feet.

This was what he had been hoping for. But was it the right ledge? For all he knew he might have taken the wrong turning at any one of a dozen places, up there among the jumbled crags. There was only one way to find out. He turned to his right and crawled on hands and knees, skirting the rubble of rocks and boulders along the base of the slope.

Suddenly his outstretched hand found nothing below it. He caught his balance and pulled back, shaken. The chill wind on his face felt as if it came from some snow-filled gulch far below.

He took a pebble from the shelf and dropped it over the edge, waiting for breathless seconds till he heard it rattle faintly, hundreds of feet down.

Had there been a precipice on one side of the ledge? Now that he thought about it he believed he could remember some such fleeting impression, as he was being rushed away from the back door of the cave.

Hastily he swung about and made a circuit in the opposite direction. After groping along for perhaps twenty yards he came to a wall of rock going up abruptly in front of him. His fingers explored its base, foot by foot. At last they found an opening a little wider than a man's body. And when he eased himself through it he knew he was in the passage that led down to the cave!

Weak, tired and bruised as he was, the boy had no thought of resting now. He pushed on as fast as his legs could carry him, falling occasionally, bumping his outthrust elbows on the irregular walls, but never stopping until the widening of the passage told him he had reached the cave itself.

Strangely enough it was here, where he had spent twenty-four hours as a captive, that his sense of direction seemed to desert him. Starting confidently toward what he thought was the center of the cave he crashed into a wall so hard it staggered him. A wave of panic swept over him then. Where was he? How could he get out of this echoing blackness where every rustle—every drip of fog moisture—whispered back at him mockingly, and nothing was where it ought to be?

He reached down an unsteady hand, found the floor and sat on it. His teeth were chattering and he had to clench his jaws to stop them. After a while he remembered the boots, still clutched in his hand. He fumbled with them and pulled one part way on his foot. When it jammed, he discovered that his thick wool sock, now a mass of rags, was causing the trouble. He ripped off the tattered remnants and was going to toss them aside. Then he remembered his red-bearded enemy, and hastily he stuffed both socks into his shirt. When the pursuit started he didn't want to leave any evidence that he had come this way.

Getting the shoes on his bare feet was a struggle, and by the time he had the laces securely tied he was almost too tired to move. Nevertheless, his panic was gone. He found he could think more clearly again.

He crawled painfully over the uneven floor till his hand touched a wall of rock. Not knowing which wall it might be, he hauled himself erect and felt his way along it. Could he be mistaken, or was the darkness actually less dense ahead? No—he could see the faint outlines of the cave mouth and feel the damp fog creeping in!

Water was falling drop by drop from the overhanging cliff above the entrance. Gratefully he tilted back his head and caught the moisture on his thirsty tongue. As he started to the left, where the ledge narrowed and the slippery path led upward to the top of the chimney, he felt himself swaying dizzily. He halted, clinging to the rock, and shook his head trying to get rid of that giddy feeling. It grew worse. He could hardly hold himself erect, and the brink of the precipice, there in the dark, only a yard from his feet, added terror to his weakness. He knew he could never reach the chimney, let alone descend it.

There was only one thing for him to do, if he wanted to escape death or recapture. That was to crawl back along the shelf, pass the cave door, and hide as best he could on the wider ledge beyond. There he hoped to steady himself and recover some of his strength.

The decision was easier to make than to carry out. The sick feeling at the pit of his stomach increased and sweat stood on his forehead even while he shivered with the cold. By plain will power he dragged himself on hands and knees along the shelf. The cave mouth yawned black on his right and he went on across it, yard by painful yard. There was one tiny corner of the ledge that was hidden from the entrance by a jutting pillar of rock. If he could make it—if he could only make it—then he would rest.

The final few feet of the distance was covered at last. He crawled into the sheltered niche and sank down on the wet stone. A vast drowsiness engulfed him.

Whether he was asleep or unconscious during those next few hours, Dick never knew. When he opened his eyes again the fog was beginning to turn gray. Morning must be at hand.

There was an ache of cold in his joints and his arms

and legs were numb from the cramped position in which he had been lying, but he felt stronger. He got up on his feet, pounding his body with his fists to restore the circulation. The dizziness was gone, and even though he was desperately hungry, he knew he was ready to tackle the chimney.

Hauling his belt a notch tighter he was in the very act of stepping out on the open ledge when a sound came from the cave mouth. A savage, hairy figure burst forth, and there stood the caveman. He held his bow and quiver in one big paw. For a second or two he stared at the wet ledge as if looking for tracks. Then he rushed away up the path to the left.

All Dick could do was to huddle back into the corner and wait, with the pounding of his heart loud in his ears.

Fourteen

AFTER HALF AN HOUR, THE WAITING became almost unbearable. Dick had no way of telling how far his bearded enemy had gone. He might be lying in wait no farther away than the chimney top. Or he might have gone down the mountain in an attempt to recapture his prisoner.

One thing seemed certain to the boy. If he went without food much longer he would never be strong enough to escape, even if he had the chance. As the minutes passed he tried to figure what the caveman would be most likely to do. First of all, why had he kept Dick a captive when it would have been so easy to kill him and drop his body over a cliff? The answer might be a key to the workings of that strange, dark, twisted mind.

There was a possibility, he thought, that the half-human brute had kept him alive on impulse, wanting some kind of companionship. But if he was now being hunted, he would surely try to get rid of his prisoner. Dick knew too much. He had seen the caveman's secret hiding place, and for that reason, if for no other, he must be disposed of.

Following that line of reasoning, Dick decided that the skin-clad giant must now be well down the mountainside. Knowing how weak his prisoner was, he would be sure he could overtake him in the valley if he had succeeded in getting that far. In the fog, the man would feel less need for caution.

Reassured by this thought, Dick resolved to leave his hidden corner and make a break for freedom. He stepped out on the shelf and went quickly past the cave entrance. Making as little noise as possible, he hurried up the winding path along the ledge. In a moment he found himself on the cliff, close to the chimney.

There was no sign of the bearded man, and no sound came from below. Yet, if he started down now, Dick knew the chances were more than even that he would meet his enemy coming up. Dared he take that desperate gamble? Or was there a safer way to do it?

Looking about him in desperation, he saw the ice cleft where the meat was cached. At least he could make sure of getting something to eat. There was still a good-sized piece of the elk haunch frozen in the snow and, pulling the arrowhead out of his pocket, he managed to hack off a strip of flesh. It was so hard he could hardly bite into it, but the taste made him ravenous. He licked his lips and thrust the cold, raw meat inside his shirt where the warmth of his body could thaw it out.

It was just at that moment that he heard a small sound —the clatter of a displaced bit of rock, somewhere far below. In sudden fear he tiptoed nearer the top of the chimney, crouched and looked down through the writhing mist. One quick glimpse showed him the shaggy figure he dreaded, striding up the trail that led along the wall of the chasm. The caveman was still a hundred feet below, but in two or three minutes he would reach the spot where Dick stood.

Panic-stricken, he pulled back from the cliff edge and stood trembling, trying frantically to think of a way out. He knew how a cornered animal must feel. His first reaction was to go back to his hiding place on the other side of the cave. But that would leave him no better off than before—sure to be discovered sooner or later.

Then a grim thought came to him. If he could find a loose stone, not too big to lift, he might throw it down at his pursuer when he got into the chimney—make him lose his hold—send him tumbling to the rocks hundreds of feet below. The picture made Dick shudder, but something had to be done, and quickly. He turned toward the rugged cliff behind him, hunting for a missile.

There was no loose stone there but he did see something else. A dozen feet up from the shelf there was a break in the rock wall—a kind of setback, above which the crag rose again precipitously. Almost as soon as his eyes could take it in, he was climbing—dragging himself up the face of the cliff with clutching hands and clinging toes.

Even if he had been in the best of condition, that would have looked to him like an impossible bit of mountaineering. Despair gave him strength—more strength than he knew he had. He went up like a frightened cat and hauled himself out on the yard-wide ledge at the top. His breath was coming in gasps, but he did his best to fill his lungs slowly and silently.

Faint, muffled sounds came up to him—shufflings and gruntings that told him his big adversary was scaling the chimney. Soon the noises were closer. The man was at the top. Dick held his breath and waited, appalled at the thought that his tracks might be discovered on the ledge. But his pursuer did not pause. The moccasined feet padded swiftly away in the direction of the cave.

Dick waited only until he was sure the man had passed the ice crevice and gone on. He might come back for meat, but first he would put his bow and arrows away in the cave, and possibly build a fire. This was the time to go.

He let himself down the cliff, took two steps across the ledge and started the descent of the chimney. If he made the slightest sound now he knew he might be trapped horribly in that dark shaft, with empty space below him and the sharp-eared gorilla-man above. So he placed his feet with utmost care and inched his way down in silence. When he got to the bottom he was half minded to take off his shoes and go barefoot in order to make less noise. But he would need the grip of the nails farther down and the time it would take him was too precious to waste. He pushed on down the ledge, moving as quietly as he could.

With every yard he advanced, Dick's fear fell away from him. For the first time since that awful moment when he first saw the bearded man face to face, he began to hope, and the feeling made him almost lightheaded. He went faster now, reckless of noise. As soon as he got out of the half darkness of the chasm he hurried down the rocky scarp, forgetful of his weakness and of the painful bruises on his battered legs. He was getting away!

The fog hid most of the mountain when he reached the green valley bottom, but he could hear no sound of pursuit. Perhaps now he could stop to satisfy that fierce gnawing in his empty stomach. The little lake was only a short distance away, and he was soon stretched on the bank, drinking thirstily of the cold water.

Next he drew the piece of meat out of his shirt and started to chew on it. As far as he knew, it was the first raw meat he had ever eaten in his life, but raw, tough and stringy as it was, it tasted good.

Before he swallowed the first mouthful, Dick was on the move again. He skirted the end of the lake, going fast through the wet, thick grass. Every few steps he turned his head, looking back over his shoulder into the mist, listening for the tread of following feet.

The sound, when he heard it, came not from behind him but from somewhere up ahead and to his right. It was the clatter of a rock tumbling down the mountainside.

He stopped where he was, his heart hammering against his ribs. Could he have gotten turned around in the fog—headed in the wrong direction when he finished drinking at the lake? With a fresh sense of panic he started to run back the way he had come, then halted again. A voice had spoken, over there near the falling rock!

"You all right, Doc?" it said.

Trembling, Dick waited for the reply, and when it came it was his father speaking.

"Yes," the botanist answered. "Thought that boulder was solid. Hope it didn't come near you."

Dick tried to yell but the words choked in his throat. He ran toward the voices, falling, picking himself up and racing on again. The rocky slope loomed out of the gray ahead, and close to the foot were two indistinct figures.

"Dad!" the boy panted hoarsely. "Dad—here I am!"

When he stumbled, a moment later, it was the husky arms of Dan Craig that caught him. And he looked up into the anxious face of his father, scrambling down the last few feet of cliff.

The ranger kept a grip on Dick's arm or he might have fallen again. All the energy that had brought him so far seemed to flow out of him, and he was weak as a day-old kitten.

The expressions on the faces of the two men almost made him laugh. Relief at finding him and shock at his appearance were mingled in their stares.

"Good grief, kid!" Craig murmured. "You look like a ghost! What happened to you?"

Dick managed a grin. "It's too long a story to tell now," he said. "We've got to get out of this valley quick. There's somebody after me." Involuntarily his frightened eyes looked back over his shoulder. "If he caught us here I think he'd kill all of us."

Craig chuckled. "Must be a pretty tough character," he said. "I'm in favor of going after him right now."

Dick shook his head. "No," he gasped. "Not without a gun! I tell you he's bad—crazy, perhaps—and he's armed. You'll need more men."

"I'll take your word for it, son," said Dr. Randolph gently. "But it's going to be a hard climb. Think you can make it? When did you eat last?"

"I forget. Yesterday, I guess it was, I had a little piece of meat. And I've been gnawing on this." He held up the strip of raw flesh.

"Ugh!" his father exclaimed with a wry face. "Here— try some of this."

Dick took the biscuit and the bar of chocolate he held out, and munched them gratefully.

"I'm all right now," he said between mouthfuls. "Let's start. I'll tell you everything when we get back to camp."

The climb took nearly two hours, for they paused often to let the boy rest. The fog began to break away just as they reached the rim, and the final lap of the journey through the basin was made in warm, sparkling sunshine.

Dick sat down on his bedroll, looked at his ragged, bloodstained shreds of clothing and laughed.

"Gosh!" he said, "I don't wonder you looked so worried when you found me!"

His father brought a pan of water and started wiping the blood from his bruised legs. "Go ahead, son," he said. "Start at the beginning."

Dick shut his eyes and drew a deep breath. "This is going to be hard for you to believe," he said. "It was for me. So don't just think I'm making it up. Let me tell you what happened and see if you can figure out the answer."

He described his descent of the snow slide and the climb from the farther edge of the valley.

"I'd gone only about ten steps from the top of the chimney," he said, "when I walked around a corner and there was this—this—well, all I can say is he looked like a Neanderthal man. He's big—way over six feet tall —with a lot of shaggy blond hair and a red beard and hairy arms and legs. He wears skins—elk and goat, I guess. The thing he hit me with was a club made out of a tree limb, but he's got a bow and arrows, too—all hand-made, of course."

Dick paused, grinning at the dubious look in Craig's eyes.

"I said you wouldn't believe it," said he. "But I was perfectly sane when I got my first look at him. He knocked me down, tied me, and lugged me back a little way to his cave."

"A white man," the ranger muttered, and shook his head. "What did he say to you? Who is he?"

"He didn't say anything. Just made a funny grunting noise, and acted as if he didn't understand me. I was about ready to believe he was some kind of leftover from the Glacial Age until yesterday when he finally spoke. It was a little past noon. He'd been out hunting and left me tied up. Then about the time he finished eating he heard a noise. Maybe it was one of you."

"It was I," said Dr. Randolph. "Dan had gone down the mountain to telephone for help, and I went over across the valley. I got up into that deep crack in the mountainside, thinking you might have had a fall. I expect I was pretty close to the chimney you speak of when I missed my footing on the wet rock and made quite a clatter. The fog was too thick to see much, so I didn't try to go up any higher."

"That must have been what he heard," Dick nodded. "Anyhow, he put out the fire, got his belongings together and grabbed me. Just as he was dragging me along to a hole in the back of the cave he said something that sounded like English—'Come on, you!' "

The boy went on to tell about the second cave, high up in the peaks, and how he had escaped during the night. The rest of the story was quickly finished.

"There's one thing I didn't mention," he said. "Do you remember whether a Navy plane was lost somewhere in the Olympics during the war?"

Craig looked thoughtful. "I wasn't here then," he said, "but I've heard some crack-ups mentioned. Why?"

Dick described the utensils and arrowheads made of aluminum alloy, and the Navy 'chute-pack. "Besides those," he said, hesitating a little, "there were three human skulls on a shelf in the cave. One of them had gold fillings in the teeth."

Craig whistled under his breath and stood up.

"Hanged if I know what you got into," he said, "but it sure sounds interesting. By the way, did this caveman fellow have a finger missing on his left hand?"

"Yes," said Dick. "I forgot to mention that. And he had our bacon, too, Dad."

The ranger was pacing up and down. "I called the Chief yesterday," he said. "He ought to be here some time tomorrow, and he'll bring along another man or two. Don't know whether they'll have guns, but we ought to be able to catch your friend, one way or another. The tough part is waiting. Tell you what, Dick. You lie there and get rested up and eat some food. Your father'll take care of you. I'll hike back to the rim and keep an eye on that valley over there. He may not show himself, now that the fog's lifted, but if he does I'll watch him through the glasses."

Fifteen

DR. RANDOLPH HELPED DICK TAKE OFF
his rags, wash the dirt out of his wounds and crawl into
the sleeping bag. Then he started some flapjacks and
heated water to make tea.

"You gave me quite a scare, son," he told the boy soberly. "That night when you didn't come back, I think
my hair must have turned a few shades grayer. I was sure
you'd had an accident, and it was all my fault—wanting

you to prove you weren't afraid. In the dark there was practically nothing I could do but keep the fire up and wait—and pray. When Craig came just after daylight, I thought it was you until he got within range of my spectacles. He wanted to go with me to hunt for you but I told him I knew just about where you'd gone and could do it myself. If you were really lost or hurt we'd need more help anyway, so he agreed to go down to the trail, where they have a telephone line."

He paused to flip a pancake. "Craig's a good man," he continued. "It's fifteen miles down to that phone box and he made it there and back before midnight. I don't believe he's slept six hours in the last two days."

Dick's eyes were on his father's haggard face. "You don't look as if you'd slept much yourself, Dad," he said.

"Come to think of it, you're right," the scientist admitted with surprise. "Soon as I've got some food into you, we'll both catch up on our rest."

They slept all that sunny afternoon. Toward dusk the ranger returned to camp. He woke them up by beating on a pan and calling them to supper.

"That Neanderthal man of yours is a cagey rascal," Craig told Dick. "He never showed himself once. I kept out of sight too, not wanting to tip him off. We may have a better chance of surprising him if he thinks he's just got you and your dad to contend with."

"I'm glad you didn't let him see you," said the boy. "I've got a kind of plan in my head—it won't work unless we get some more fog, though."

"What's the plan?" asked Craig. "Let's hear it."

"I haven't thought it through yet, but—well—if there's a heavy fog, so we could get over there without his spotting us, I'd go out as a sort of decoy. The way he acted, the last time I saw him, he doesn't like the idea of my getting away. I believe he might come out after me."

"Sounds good to me," the ranger said. "A strong, fast-moving chap like that would be hard to catch in a straightaway chase. We'll have to outsmart him one way or another."

Dr. Randolph finished his meal and stood up. "One thing that occurs to me," he said, "is that this strange creature may come prowling over this way tonight. You and I have had some sleep, son. I suggest we stand watch, taking turn and turn about. That will give Dan a real night's rest for a change."

They overruled Craig's objections to the arrangement, and Dick took the first watch. He kept the fire up, sitting close to it, reveling in its warmth. The ax lay a foot from his hand, ready in case a weapon should be needed.

The hours passed peacefully enough. He succeeded in staying awake by going over his adventure detail by detail, trying to fix the position of everything in the cave and around it clearly in his mind.

A little after twelve he shook his father's shoulder and woke him up. Then he crawled into the eiderdown and was almost instantly asleep.

Dick was the last one up in the morning. The ranger and his father were standing by the fire, dim gray shapes in the mist. They were talking cheerfully, in low voices, and he could tell from their conversation that the camp had not been disturbed.

"Well, son," said the botanist, when he joined them, "you've got your wish as far as fog is concerned. Now if Chief Ranger Campbell gets here we can give your plan a trial."

There was a sizzle of bacon in the pan. Craig had brought a small quantity of it in his pack, and there was enough left to give them each a single crisp slice.

"Save that grease," Dick told the ranger. "I'll go get us a trout to cook in it."

"You'll get us a what? I'm afraid you won't find any trout in these lakes."

Dick chuckled. "I guess Dad's had too much on his mind to tell you. That's another of our mysteries. Big, handsome rainbows just waiting for your bait!"

The young man scratched his head in bafflement. "But," he said, "it's a physical impossibility for fish to get up here. I've seen that fall at the outlet of the lakes. It's higher'n a church steeple."

"You'll believe it, all right," Dick laughed. "Come on down and I'll show you. I don't know how they got here, unless somebody brought 'em up the mountain. Say—you don't suppose—"

Craig nodded. "Your caveman, you mean? Sounds reasonable. He seems to have made himself pretty much at home up in this country. Let's see whether the trout'll bite in the fog."

Dick turned over stones till he had three or four white grubs and led the way down the meadow to the second lake. When they reached the point of rocks he handed the pole to the ranger.

"Try it yourself," he suggested.

Craig cast half a dozen times without getting a nibble. Then a good-sized fish took the lure. There was a ten-minute battle that tested all the ranger's skill, but he finally flipped the trout out on the bank. He put on another grub and went on fishing. Inside of an hour they were on their way back to camp with three trout, all over fifteen inches.

They could hear voices before they were able to see the stunted trees through the fog.

"That must be the Chief Ranger," said Craig, hurrying his steps. "Golly—he sure made time getting here!"

There were three men standing around the fire when the fishermen reached the place. Dick saw Campbell's spare figure beside his father, and another man, tall and lanky, dressed in woodsman's clothes.

Craig greeted his boss and took a playful swipe at the other ranger. "Slim!" he exclaimed. "Haven't seen you in months. Where'd you drop from?"

The tall man grinned good-naturedly. "Why, you ol' hoss-thief!" said he. "It's too dang long since we got together. Me, I been up north on the upper Soleduck. Jus' happened to report in at headquarters day before yesterday, an' I was the only man the Chief could get his hands on in a hurry."

"Well, boys," said Campbell, "we've got some business to attend to. Dick Randolph, this is Slim Harvey. Used to be a cowhand over in Oregon, and grew up with the idea he couldn't go any place except on a horse. He's been cured, though. I had to hustle to stay with him, on the hike up here.

"Dr. Randolph's given us a rough idea of what you ran into, Dick, and we're mighty glad to find you back here safe. Now suppose you fill in the details, so we'll know just what we're up against."

The boy went over his story again, pausing now and then to answer the Chief Ranger's questions.

"You're sure those metal things in the cave were made out of airplane aluminum?" Campbell asked. "And the letters 'U. S. Navy' were on the parachute-pack? Because that explains several things. Back in the winter of 'forty-four, we got a report from the Navy that a twin-engine transport was missing. It had been flying up the coast from San Diego and they figured it might have run into icing conditions in a storm above these mountains. They had search planes going over for a week, and we guided ground parties that were hunting for it, too. Nobody ever found so much as a scrap of wreckage.

"As near as I can remember, they told us there were

five men aboard the plane—two pilots, a radio man, an armed guard and a prisoner of war. This prisoner was something special. He was a gunner's mate on a U-boat, and he'd broken out of two prison camps before they finally found him working in a shipyard somewhere in California. The Navy didn't broadcast any description of him, but a Lieutenant Commander in charge of one of the search parties told me a few things, off the record. How big would you say your cave dweller was?"

"He's a full head taller than I," said Dick. "At least four or five inches over six feet, I should think, and built like a Chicago Bears' tackle. At a guess, he must weigh two hundred and fifty."

Slim Harvey gave a low whistle, but the Chief Ranger merely nodded.

"That checks," he said. "The three skulls you saw in the cave are interesting, too. If my theory's right, there ought to be four, but it really doesn't make much difference. It's likely he never found the other man. You see what I'm getting at? First of all, we can throw out the idea that this fellow is a hand-me-down from the Ice Age. That's what he's trying to act like, but it's a fairly safe bet that he's an ordinary man with a mighty good reason for hiding out up here.

"Now let's see how that fits our big Nazi war prisoner, supposedly killed in a plane crash. One other thing that officer told me was that before they captured him, down there in California, he hit one of their men over the head with a rivet gun and the poor chap died, a few days later. So there's a charge of murder hanging over him, in addition to everything else."

Craig nodded. "That ought to be reason enough," he said. "What I couldn't figure till now was why anybody would be willing to live like an animal in a cave—unless, of course, he was plain crazy."

"Hm-m," said Slim Harvey, half closing one eye, "I seem to see some right lively action comin' our way. When do we start?"

"I'd say it better be pretty soon," replied the Chief Ranger. "This fog may not last more than another hour. Think we could get over there in that time, Dick?"

"Yes, sir. There's a long snow slide into the valley and we can glissade down. But I'd like to suggest a plan— something I told Dan about. You see, this caveman is going to get away if he can. He's quick as a cat, and he knows all the peaks and canyons and hiding places for miles around. I'm afraid if he heard us coming he'd just vanish and it would take an army to dig him out. You'd be lucky to get a long-range shot at him, and I guess you'd rather take him alive, wouldn't you?"

"That's right," said Campbell. "What's your idea?"

"Well," the boy told him, "I don't believe he knows yet that he's got more than two people to deal with—Dad and me. If we could all get over there before the fog lifts I thought you three could hide, up on the side of the mountain. There's a deep, narrow crack in the cliff that leads way back to the chimney. I thought I'd go up in there and yell for help, as if I'd had a fall or something. Dad could answer from down below. This German—if that's who he is—must understand English. And I'm pretty sure he could hear me if I hollered loud enough. Now he figures Dad and I are the only two people who know he's there. Why wouldn't he try to get us both out of the way? Suppose he comes down after me and chases me out onto the open slope, where you're waiting. Isn't that our best chance to surprise him?"

Campbell nodded and Harvey grinned his approval. The lanky ex-cowboy went briskly over to his pack and took out a coil of half-inch rope.

"Figured we might need this for some tricky climbin'," he said. "Now it looks like I might have a better use for it."

With strong, deft fingers he raveled the strands at one end and spliced them back into the rope to form the "eye" of a noose. When it was as firmly anchored as the rope itself, he passed the free end through the opening, made his loop, gathered the coils in his left hand and started a lazy-looking spin with his right.

Dick was standing some twenty feet away. Suddenly, with no apparent effort on Slim's part, the loop sailed out over the boy's head and the next instant he felt his arms tightly pinioned to his sides.

For a few seconds he was too surprised to join in the laughter of the others. Then he grinned delightedly.

"Man!" he exclaimed. "You're good with that thing! I'd like to see old Red-beard's face if you can get close enough to rope him!"

Alec Campbell looked at his watch. "I guess we're ready," he said. "Let's go."

Dick got his camera and gave it to his father. "Would you mind carrying this, Dad?" he asked. "There might be a chance for some pictures if we're lucky. I've used up all the color film but black and white's better than nothing."

The boy was dressed in the same ragged clothes he had worn when he escaped. Now, as they passed the first lake, he picked up a handful of mud and smeared it in patches on his arms, legs and face.

"If I'm going to put on an act," he said, "I might as well look the part."

"You do," Craig assured him. "You'd pass for the last survivor in a shipwreck movie."

They were hurrying along the shore of the third lake when they heard a loud splash, off to the right in the fog.

"Hey! What was that?" asked Campbell. "Sounded like a fish jumping."

"That's what it was," Craig told him. "I guess you didn't notice the three trout Dick and I brought back this morning. We think this caveman must have stocked the lake."

The Chief Ranger's face was grim. "He's done pretty well for himself," he commented. "Plenty of fresh meat —fish—makes us look a little silly, doesn't it? I'm going to enjoy getting my hands on that Hitler-heiling kraut."

Sixteen

THE MIST OVERHEAD WAS BEGINNING TO
break as they climbed the northwest bastion of the rim,
and Campbell urged them to make speed.

They reached the ledge and rounded the corner where
they could look down into the valley. Dick was in the
lead.

"It's all right," he said in a low voice. "The fog's still
thick down below. Here's the top of the slide."

He waited till they were all assembled, then stepped out confidently to start his glissade. It went smoothly enough for the first hundred yards. Then, just as he was gathering speed one of his nailed boots caught for an instant, twisting his leg under him. He was shooting down on his side, the wet ice biting cold through the rents in his clothes.

When he struck the swampy ground at the bottom there was no breath left in him. Gasping, he hauled himself to his feet and hobbled a few yards. One after another the rest of the party came swishing down and landed sprawling in the water-soaked grass.

Campbell got up, shaking himself like a dog. "Can't say much for that, except it's quick," he growled. "Everybody all right?"

Dick grinned wryly. "I won't have to fake a limp," he replied. "Turned my ankle on the way down. It's nothing serious, though."

He pushed on across the valley at the best speed he could make, and gradually his ankle grew less painful. The fog was lifting now. They could see the lake and the timber at the head of the valley, but there was still a gray blanket above them, concealing their movements from any eyes that might be watching on the opposite mountain.

There was no more talk. They climbed the first cliff in silence and went toiling up the zigzag trail among the rocks.

After a few hundred yards, Dick motioned to his father. "You'd better stay down here, Dad," he whispered. "When you hear me call you can start on up, as if you were hunting for me."

The rest continued the climb until they were close to the mouth of the chasm. The Chief Ranger, with his big service automatic strapped to his hip, took his station under the overhang of an outcropping ledge. Craig found a hiding place behind a boulder a few yards higher.

Dick and Slim Harvey went on till they reached the entrance of the rock cleft. There the lanky ranger moved aside a step or two and stood with his back to the cliff. He held the coiled rope loosely in his hands.

"Good luck!" he whispered, and Dick smiled his thanks. A moment later he was limping up the ledge in the deepening gloom of the chasm.

It was so quiet that the crunch of his nailed boots on the stone echoed hollowly between the dark walls. He went more slowly, trying to walk without noise. At last the narrowest and most treacherous part of the trail lay just ahead of him, with the foot of the chimney in sight, beyond. If he went any farther he would have to cling to the cliff with his hands, and in an emergency it would take him time to get out. He decided to stay where he was.

There was no need to pretend a quaver in his voice when he gave his first yell. Excitement tightened his throat and made the sound hoarse and strained.

"Help!" he shouted. "Da-a-d! Help! I've hurt my-self!"

He kept it up at intervals, making a megaphone of his hands and yelling toward the top of the cleft. After a few shouts he heard a faint reply from outside.

"Dick!" his father was calling. "Where are you? Can you hear me?"

"Yes," he bellowed. "I'm up here, Dad! I fell and hurt my leg! Help!"

"All right," came the answer. "Stay where you are. Don't try to move. I'm coming!"

Crouching there on the ledge, the boy kept his eyes on the slit of light at the top of the chasm. If the caveman had heard him, he would have had time to get there by now.

From the spot where he waited, the chimney itself was hidden by a bulge in the chasm wall. Dick realized, with an uneasy feeling, that his enemy might already be descending the shaft. He straightened up apprehensively, staring at the jutting rock that cut off his view. And in that split second he saw the shaggy head of the caveman appear around its edge, only forty feet away.

Choking back a cry of terror, the boy turned and darted down the sloping ledge. He forgot his weak ankle and everything else in the blind urge to get away. Before he had taken a dozen strides he tripped and fell to his knees. It was a lucky accident, for at that instant an arrow whizzed viciously past, a foot above his head. It glanced off the rock just beyond him and went clattering down into the chasm.

Dick picked himself up and dashed on. The bearded giant wasn't taking time to fit another arrow to the bow. His thudding footfalls were loud in the boy's ears as he came in hot pursuit.

Trying to remember the chase afterward, Dick found it hard to believe that he had taken the twists and turns of that slanting ledge at such breakneck speed. Yet he must have run all the way, for he was still half a dozen strides in the lead when he came out on the mountainside at the foot of the chasm.

Just as he left the opening he stumbled and pitched forward, rolling twenty feet down the steep slope before he brought up against a boulder. Bruised and dizzy, he cowered there, expecting to see his huge foe charging after him.

Instead of that, the caveman had halted a step or two outside the entrance, glaring about him as if he suspected a trick. Dick looked up in time to see the loop of Slim Harvey's rope settle over the giant's shoulders and twitch tight, clamping his hairy arms to his sides.

There was a yell of triumph from the ex-cowboy and a roar of baffled rage from his victim. For a wild moment the bearded man wrestled mightily to break the hold of the rope. Then he succeeded in getting a hand on the hilt of the hunting knife at his waist and tugged it out of the sheath.

"Look out!" cried Dick. "He's going to cut himself loose!"

AT THAT INSTANT AN ARROW WHIZZED VICIOUSLY PAST

But Slim was already in action. He had jumped down the hill before the boy's warning shout. Now, with a quick jerk on the rope, he threw the caveman off balance and brought him tumbling down the rough slope. The knife spun out of his hand, falling a few feet away, and Dick picked it up.

Craig and Campbell were on the scene now. The younger ranger dove in recklessly and tried to pin the giant to the ground, but he was tossed aside by a thrashing heave of those powerful legs.

"Here," said the Chief Ranger calmly, "no use getting hurt. His life isn't worth it."

He leveled his forty-five at the caveman's head and barked an order in German.

"Achtung!" he said. "Lie still where you are or I'll shoot you dead!"

The effect of his words was immediate. The big man stopped struggling and blinked as he looked into the muzzle of the gun. Campbell nudged him with his toe.

"Turn over," he commanded. "On your stomach. Hands behind you. *Macht es schnell!"*

The giant rolled over obediently and in a few seconds Harvey had lashed his wrists solidly together with the free end of the rope.

Dick heard footsteps and saw his father hurrying up the hill.

"It worked, Dad!" he cried. "We've got him safe. Gosh! Let me have that camera!"

Dr. Randolph unbuckled the case from his belt and in a moment the boy was setting the adjustments. The camera, he was glad to find, had suffered no damage during the descent of the snow slide.

"Get up!" Campbell snapped at his prisoner. "Up! On your feet!"

The man in skins twisted to a sitting position, got his knees under him and staggered up. He stood there in the sunlight, glowering at them sullenly from under shaggy brows.

Dick caught the pose in the finder and clicked the shutter. With a snarl, the giant took a step toward him, straining against the rope that bound his hands. Apparently he didn't like cameras. The boy turned the film quickly and got a close-up shot of that threatening, brutish face before Slim Harvey could yank the prisoner back to his place.

The Chief Ranger handed his pistol to Dan Craig.

"I want to go up and have a look at that cave," he said. "You and Slim take him down to the valley and wait for Dick and me. You know how to handle a gun. Use it on him if he tries any funny business."

Dick put the camera back in the case and strapped it to his belt. Then he followed Campbell toward the entrance of the cleft.

"How's your ankle?" asked the Chief. "Better not try the climb if it hurts you."

"It seems to be getting better all the time," Dick replied cheerfully. "You saw me come tearing out of here. I had to run on it then, and I guess that did me good. It isn't a sprain, anyhow."

Campbell paused at the break in the cliff and examined the bow and arrows that lay where the caveman had dropped them.

"We'll take those along on our way back," he said. "With a bow like that I can see how he could kill an elk."

Dick told him how close he had come to having an arrow through his back, half an hour earlier.

"There was nothing wrong with his aim," the boy said. "Just by plain chance and clumsiness I fell down and it missed me. Whew! Did I start moving then!"

They reached the chimney and worked their way up without too much difficulty. At the meat cache the Chief Ranger pulled out what was left of the elk haunch and held it while Dick took a picture. Then they went on to the cave.

While Campbell was looking around inside, the boy made other shots—two of the ledge and the cave mouth, and two more of the wild, snowy peaks to the westward. The last shreds of fog had disappeared now and the sun was shining brightly.

When the Chief Ranger reappeared he was dragging a number of things out to the light. On the shelf in front of the cavern he made a pile of them—the water basin and skillet, the skis, the three grinning skulls, the parachute-pack and the goatskin, besides a worn-out moccasin and the broken blade of a knife, hammered out of dural-umin.

In his hand Campbell held several pieces of rawhide thong.

"Reckon we can make a bundle of these things and let 'em down the chimney," he said.

They tied the shaggy white skin around the other items and attached a long thong to it. Then Dick climbed down to the ledge below the chimney and pulled the bundle in when Campbell lowered it slowly within his reach. It made an awkward burden to carry on the first and narrowest part of the trail, but the grizzled mountaineer balanced it skillfully across his shoulder and held on to the rock with one hand.

When they were outside the chasm, Dick picked up the big bow and the quiver of arrows and they went on down the mountain. In the distance, at the farther side of the green valley floor, they could see four figures, toiling insect-like up the rocky scarp.

The Chief Ranger smiled. "For a pre-historic caveman," he said, "our big friend seems to have an uncanny instinct about guns. He'll go along like a lamb as long as Craig keeps him covered."

"He sure jumped when you hollered at him in German," Dick remarked. "You must have heard that word *'Achtung'* used before. It means something like 'Attention' or 'Listen' in English, doesn't it?"

"That's close to it," said Campbell. "I picked the word up at Château-Thierry, back in 'eighteen. We used to shout it whenever we were handling kraut prisoners, and it still seems to work."

They crossed the grassy width of the valley and began the long ascent. In spite of the load he carried, the Chief Ranger climbed at a steady pace, and Dick was hard pressed to keep up with him.

They were nearing the top when they overtook the other members of the party and their prisoner.

"It's been slow going, Chief," said Craig apologetically. "We didn't want to untie his hands, and that's why we couldn't push him too fast. Here—let me pack that stuff the rest of the way."

Campbell took the gun and turned over his bulky bundle to the younger ranger. It was past noon when they mounted the rim and came down again into Four Lakes Basin.

"I don't know about the rest of you," said the Chief Ranger, "but speaking for myself, I'm hungry. Slim and I were traveling fast on light rations, and the breakfast we ate at five this morning wasn't what you'd call filling."

Slim Harvey grinned. "I'll second the Chief on that," he drawled. "S'pose I lope on ahead an' get some grub cookin'. Dick, maybe you'd like to play horse with this hunk o' man for a while."

He handed the boy the end of the rope that bound their captive's wrists and went off up the meadow at a swinging trot.

Dick watched the great hulking shoulders and bowed head in front of him, and wondered what was going on under that matted thatch of hair. The caveman was no fool. If, as all the evidence seemed to indicate, he was the Nazi prisoner who had been aboard the lost Navy plane, he must realize that his present case was desperate. Was he planning an escape even now? The boy had more reason to respect his brute strength and cunning than any of the others in the party. He shivered as he thought of what the giant might do if the slightest chance offered itself. And then and there he resolved that whatever happened he would not be caught napping.

Seventeen

THEY COULD SEE A CHEERFUL SPIRE OF
smoke rising from the cooking fire as they drew near the
Randolphs' camp.

"Wonder if Slim found those trout," Dan Craig remarked. "I hung 'em under a tree, so they ought to be
fresh enough, and with six mouths to feed, they'll be
needed."

"That's a fact," said Campbell. "If I'd had my wits

about me I'd have brought along that chunk of elk meat we saw up by the cave. Slim and I only packed about five days' grub, and I suppose you're running short, too. How are your supplies holding out, Dr. Randolph?"

"We've a little left," the botanist replied, "but of course our bacon was stolen. What we've got is mostly flour, with a little dried milk, some tea and a few bars of chocolate."

"Well, we'll just have to make it do," said the Chief Ranger. "As soon as we've had a meal we'll pack up and start. There's enough food for one day more, anyway. We'll push along as fast as we can, and try to reach the Dosewallips before anybody starves."

Harvey proved to be as adept with a skillet as he was with a rope. He had the fish cleaned and was rolling them in corn meal when the others arrived on the scene. Fifteen minutes later they were all eating except the prisoner. He had refused with a surly shake of his head when Craig offered to feed him a piece of fish.

"Listen, Heinie," said Campbell, eyeing the giant coldly. "It makes no difference to us whether you eat or not. You're going to do a lot of traveling in the next two days, so if you're wise you'll keep in shape for it. Also, it seems to me, it's time for you to be a little more sociable. What's your name?"

There was no answer, nor any visible expression on the savage, hairy face.

"You understand German well enough," the Chief

Ranger continued, "and I think you know some English, too. You don't gain a thing by acting dumb. What's your name? *Wie heisst du?*"

The question brought only the same blank glare from the man's piglike eyes.

"All right," snapped Campbell. "I'll tell you who you are. Your name's Dortner—Anton Dortner. As soon as we get down the mountain we'll shave off that beard and give you a crew haircut, so the Navy Intelligence men can take a good look at you."

The caveman's scowl deepened but he still kept his mouth shut. Campbell shrugged his shoulders and turned away.

"Everybody through eating?" he asked. "Let's pack, then, and get started. We've still got five or six hours of daylight and I'd like to make it all the way down to the trail before we camp."

Dick laid out his own pack and his father's and began piling the duffel beside them. He had thought there would be little to carry on the homeward trip, for they had eaten up most of their supply of food. Now, as he eyed the mounting heap, he began to wonder.

There were his marmot skins, each on its stretcher, to add bulk to the load. He wrapped them carefully in paper he had saved for the purpose, then gave them still more protection by folding them inside his spare clothing. The pots and pans, flour-bag and camp ax filled the knapsack almost to overflowing. He found room in a snug corner for his exposed film and topped the load off with his bedroll.

Dr. Randolph's pack was less of a problem. Although he had collected several hundred plants, they added little weight to the specimen-boxes. And the books he had filled with his neatly written notes were no heavier than when he brought them up the mountain.

Alec Campbell, meanwhile, was dividing the caveman's belongings among the other three packs.

"This junk is heavy and awkward to carry," he told Craig and Harvey, "but it's important. Those skulls, for instance—they're not just souvenirs. The Navy or the F.B.I. can probably tell who they belonged to from the dental work. We'll let the prisoner lug some of the stuff— just hang those skis and the water-pot around his neck."

They were ready in half an hour. Dick, waiting till the little procession had strung out in single file and headed for the south rim, took a final look behind him. Four Lakes Basin lay wild and peaceful in the afternoon light. Except for the blackened stone of the fireplace he had built, the great meadow looked as if no human foot had ever trod its flowery expanse.

The boy pursed his lips and whistled, grinning as he heard the marmots' lively answering chorus. He was glad to think that henceforth the little mountain colony would live undisturbed. At last he turned and hurried after his companions.

.   .   .

Downhill work with a pack, Dick soon discovered, was not as easy as he had imagined. The snow slide up which they had toiled when they first approached the basin looked invitingly smooth. Without those burdens on their backs they could have made it in a quick glissade. As it was they had to go down step by careful step.

Next came the long, rocky hogback, traversed by game trails. It had taken most of a morning to climb, on the way up, but the descent was made steadily, without rests. In two hours they had reached the partly wooded meadow where Dick had photographed the bull elk.

Until that time he had kept up with the others without difficulty. Now his ankle began to tire and he could not conceal the limp that came with each step.

Dr. Randolph looked back and noticed the painful hitch in his gait.

"Take it easy, son," he told him. "I'll stay with you and we'll rest a bit. Campbell's anxious to get down to the nearest telephone box so he can get word through to the Bremerton Navy Yard about his prisoner. But that doesn't mean we have to keep up with them."

They sat down on a fallen log near the elk trail they were following. Dick rubbed his ankle as best he could without taking the boot off. He knew the joint would stiffen and swell up if he untied the laces, and he thought it was better to keep it tightly bound as long as he had to walk on it.

The Chief Ranger discovered they had dropped behind and came back to them while the others waited.

"I'm ashamed of myself, Dick," he apologized. "I'd honestly forgotten all about that ankle of yours. But with so little food left I'm afraid we'll have to keep going till nightfall, anyway. Or—wait—I've got it. The rest of you can camp at the head of the pass, just beyond this meadow. From there it's only a couple of hours to the trail and I'll go on down and put in my call. If Joe Evans is at the main camp, I'll have him start somebody up with a pack-load of grub to meet us. Then we won't have to push along so fast."

"You don't have to worry about me," Dick told him stoutly. "All I need is a few minutes' rest. Then I can make it down to the pass easy. I remember the place. We camped there on the way up. It's only a couple of miles more."

Campbell grinned. "I like your spunk," he said. "We'll make a ranger out of you, if you don't watch out. Take your time. I'll tell Craig to wait for you."

With that he was gone, striding off down the meadow as if his big pack weighed no more than a feather pillow.

Dick and his father sat there for another twenty minutes, then made a fresh start. The rest had helped, and the boy found that by going slowly he could travel without too many twinges. Late in the afternoon the party passed the spring, where Dick had first seen the giant handprint in the mud. He looked ahead at the slouching figure of the caveman but the big fellow gave no sign that he remembered that night.

Craig led the way over a rise and set down his pack at the foot of the twisted old evergreen that stood in the crest of the saddle. It was the same spot where they had camped, the night before they reached Four Lakes Basin.

Harvey removed the skis and the big aluminum basin from their prisoner's shoulders and motioned to him to sit down.

"I'll build the fire, Dan," he said, "if you'll go back to the spring after water. Here, Doc, you take the gun an' keep ol' whiskers in line."

Dr. Randolph handled the big black automatic gingerly. Dick was glad the safety catch was on, as he watched the uncertain waving of the muzzle.

"Wait till I get this shoe off, Dad," he chuckled. "Then you'd better let me have the artillery and we'll all feel safer."

Slim Harvey concocted such a meal as he could from their scanty provisions, and everyone except the caveman ate with a good appetite. By the time darkness fell they were ready to turn in.

"Reckon we'll have to stand watches," Craig told the lanky ex-cowboy. "But if you hog-tie this critter I don't believe he'll make any trouble."

Harvey looked over the knots on the bearded man's wrists and threw a few expert hitches around his ankles as well.

"All secure," he announced. "Got a quarter in your

pocket? I'll flip you for the first watch. Heads, you say? Tails it is. I'll wake you up, come midnight."

Craig and the Randolphs crawled into their sleeping bags. The other ranger buckled the holstered automatic to his waist, threw the goatskin robe over the prisoner and squatted, cross-legged, in front of the fire.

Dick was tired enough, but he did not go to sleep at once. His ankle, relieved of the pressure of the laced boot, had begun to puff up and throb. He rubbed it with his hands as best he could without getting out of the warm eiderdown. It felt somewhat better after that, and in a short time he drowsed off.

Two or three hours must have passed before he woke again. Perhaps he had turned over in his sleep and given the swollen ankle a twist. At any rate, it was hurting him again.

Overhead, through the branches of the old hemlock a pale half moon had broken through the clouds. It shed a cold light over the misty peaks, the broad rock ledge and the embers of the dying fire. It shone, too, on the dark, still figures of the sleeping men. Slim Harvey's chin had fallen forward on his chest, and he was snoring gently.

Dick turned his head to look toward the shaggy bundle that lay between his father and Dan Craig. His first glance reassured him. The huge body was still where it should be. But even as he watched there was a twitching, heaving motion under the goat hide. The hairy skin was suddenly flung aside and in an instant the giant was standing in a crouch, arms and legs unbound, flexing his great hands. He was not looking toward the boy. His whole attention was riveted on the gun at Harvey's hip as he took a noiseless step forward.

Dick choked back the shout that had sprung to his lips. He sat up, wriggling silently to free himself from the sleeping bag. By the time he got his feet out, the caveman's stealthy advance had brought him within a stride of the sleeping ranger.

The boy looked around him, hunting desperately for a weapon. The ax was out of his reach, tucked under the flap of his pack. As he gathered his stockinged feet under him and put out a hand to lift himself, he touched a loose rock. It was rough-edged and heavy, bigger than his fist. In a flash his fingers wrapped themselves around the stone. He stood up, his swollen ankle forgotten, and drew back his pitching arm.

A dozen feet away the caveman stooped, jerked the automatic out of its holster and whirled erect. He held the gun as if his hairy paw was used to such weapons. Dick saw his thumb flick off the safety catch, as those fierce little eyes swung from Harvey toward Craig. With all his strength the boy hurled the rock straight at the caveman's head.

It struck with a muffled thump just above the giant's shaggy temple and he went down like a falling tree.

Dick had no idea whether he had knocked him out.

He only knew he had to get that gun. In a frantic dive he landed across the huge, outstretched arm and tore the automatic out of the man's loosened fingers.

"Slim!" he yelled. "Dan! Give me a hand with this guy!"

"Huh?" mumbled Harvey, scrambling to his feet. "What—good gosh! What's been goin' on here?"

Craig was up, too, and Dr. Randolph. They stood in an awed circle, staring down at the still, sprawled figure of the caveman and at the boy, sitting beside him, holding the gun.

Dick broke the silence with a giggle. Their open-mouthed astonishment struck him as funny, now that it was over.

"Sorry," he said. "Guess I didn't need to wake you all up. I hit him with a rock and he seems to be out pretty cold."

Harvey knelt quickly and put his hand under the ragged skins on the man's left side.

"The big lug's lucky," he muttered. "His heart's beatin'. Doggone my lazy hide! What made me go to sleep on watch? Reckon I was too sure o' those knots I'd tied him with."

He went to the spot where the man had lain and brought back the rope. A frazzled end told the story. The giant had chafed it part way through on the rocks, then broken it by main strength.

"Well, he won't get out o' this one," said the ex-cowboy

WITH ALL HIS STRENGTH THE BOY HURLED THE ROCK

grimly, as he pulled the unresisting wrists back into position and whipped the cord around them.

Dick's father had gone to his pack for the flashlight.
Now he pushed up the tangled hair on the big man's head.
There was an ugly-looking bruise, from which the dark
blood oozed slowly.

"If you'll get me some water," said the scientist, "I
think we'd better wash this wound and bandage it."

Craig hurried off to the spring and Harvey put fresh
kindling on the coals of the fire. Under Dr. Randolph's
careful hands the blood was sponged away with warm
water and a strip torn from a clean shirt was bound
around the unconscious man's head.

"I can't be sure," the botanist told them, "but I don't
believe there's any fracture of the skull. That thick shock
of hair probably saved his life. Nothing more we can do
for him that I can see. We may as well go back to bed."

As Dick crept into the sleeping bag once more it wasn't
just the chill of the mountain night that made him shiver.
He realized for the first time how close he had come to
killing a man.

Eighteen

BEFORE SUNRISE DAN CRAIG WOKE THE
sleeping camp with the sharp ring of ax strokes, as he
cut wood for a breakfast fire. It seemed to Dick as if
the night had been extra short. He yawned, rubbed the
sleep out of his eyes and rolled over, blinking at the other
figures on the ledge. He saw his father get out of his
eiderdown and kneel beside the prisoner.

"So," he said, "he's come to, has he? I see the wound's

stopped bleeding, too. Shouldn't wonder if he'd be ready to travel."

He turned toward Dick. "How's your ankle, son?"

The boy reached down inside the sleeping bag and felt of the injured joint.

"Doesn't seem to be swollen so much," he answered. "And I can move it all right. I can tell you better when I walk on it."

He got up and took a few cautious steps. "It's okay," he reported. "I'll hardly feel it, once I get my boot on."

They ate flapjacks and drank tea. To everybody's surprise the caveman meekly accepted the food Slim Harvey offered him. With his legs unbound so that he could sit up, he leaned forward, eager to gulp the hot liquid held to his mouth. And half a dozen pancakes were hardly enough to satisfy his appetite.

"Reckon you aim to behave yourself now," the lanky ranger remarked, in much the same tone he would use if he were talking to a horse. "That crack on the head must have knocked some sense into you. Come on, you've had enough. Let's get movin'."

They shouldered their packs and got under way again. The first beams of sun were turning the western peaks from gray to rosy gold as they went down the rough scarp. Dick had laced his boots tightly and by the time he had walked the first stiffness out of his ankle, it felt almost as strong as ever. He was able to enjoy the beauty of the morning without qualms.

Two or three hours after the start they reached the cliff where Dick and his father had rested during the upward climb. Here it was necessary to untie the prisoner's hands before he could descend. Slim Harvey went down first, and kept the big man covered with the automatic. Then the others followed. At the foot of the crag they bound their captive's wrists once more and continued on down the narrow ridge of the cleaver.

There was thick timber a hundred feet below them on either side. Craig saw the prisoner eyeing those dense hemlock thickets and stepped close to his elbow.

"Don't get funny ideas, brother," he said. "You wouldn't go ten yards before you stopped a forty-five slug. That man Slim killed quite a few of your Nazi friends when he was in the Army, and I bet he wouldn't mind shooting one more, even if the war *is* over."

The big man halted suddenly and swung about to face the ranger. A look of bewilderment was in his eyes.

"Der war," he said stumblingly. "You say it iss over? No more fighting?"

"That's right, Heinie. Been over for two years. We licked you proper this time, too."

"But—" stammered the German, "der Fuehrer!"

Craig shook his head. "Hitler's dead," he announced calmly. "Committed suicide the day Berlin fell. And by the way—now that you've started talking—what's your name? You're Dortner, aren't you?"

The giant's eyes narrowed and he shrugged his huge

shoulders. "I don't talk," he replied and shut up like a clam.

At the lower end of the ridge they came to the ranger trail, leading up from the blueberry meadows below, and heading northwest along the saddle. Sitting comfortably under a tree beside a telephone box was the Chief Ranger. He got up and came toward them.

"What's been going on?" he asked, as he saw the bloody bandage around the prisoner's head.

Slim Harvey grinned. "You can blame me, Chief. I ought to be court-martialed. Figured I had him tied so he was safe last night, an' went sound asleep. He worked loose an' got my gun, all set for a massacre. We'd have been in bad shape if Dick, here, hadn't pitched a strike with a rock. Knocked him cold as a fish."

"Hm," said Campbell. "David and Goliath, eh? It's a fine thing when you big he-rangers have to be protected by a tenderfoot, and a boy at that!"

He went back to the tree and picked up a bark basket, filled with blueberries. "I knew you folks were on short rations," he said with a twinkle. "These'll do you good. Balance your diet. I picked 'em while I was waiting for you, this morning."

Dick was glad to sit on a log and rest for a few minutes. His ankle was holding up well, but it had been a tiring morning. He munched gratefully on a double handful of berries and looked off at the panorama of the peaks. It was the last time he would see them from such a vantage point—on this trip at least. Some day, he vowed, he would come back, and bring plenty of color film with him. This was his kind of country.

"I got Joe Evans by phone last night," the Chief Ranger was saying. "He'd come over to take charge while I was up here, and by good luck Bill Cleveland got in from his patrol yesterday. Bill was going to make an early start this morning with a pack of grub. If we keep pushing we'll meet him down the trail in time for a good supper. So tighten your belts, boys, and let's get at it."

They scrambled down the steep, rocky head wall of the blueberry valley and plowed through miles of brush at a steady pace. By mid-afternoon they reached the bank of a swift-flowing mountain stream just above the place where it plunged over the cliff into the canyon below. Dick remembered the spot well, for it was on this part of the trail that he had taken his pictures of the waterfall.

The descent along the canyon's side was slower going. In places they had to slide and cling to the roots of mountain hemlocks that thrust out from the almost perpendicular wall. Farther down there was dense brush to fight. The sun had settled behind the western rim and the canyon lay in shadow before they came at last to the lean-to on the upper reaches of the Dosewallips.

There was a thin spire of smoke rising from beyond the shelter, and a man stood in the glow of the cooking fire.

"Hiya, folks," he called cheerfully. "Lay off your packs an' take a breather. Grub's most ready."

He was introduced by the Chief Ranger as Bill Cleveland. When he had shaken hands with the Randolphs he turned to stare at the prisoner with lively curiosity.

"Hear you caught the wild man o' Borneo in person," he grinned. "Boy! He's no pygmy, is he? What's he live on—raw meat?"

"That's what he's been eatin' lately," Slim Harvey drawled. "But we sort o' figure he grew up on sauerkraut an' wieners. Anyhow he's still tryin' to get used to the idea that the super-race lost the war."

Hungry as they all were, that was a meal to remember. There were slabs of sizzling steak and fried potatoes. There were warmed-up biscuits, made by Fong Yee the night before, and real butter and preserves. And to top it off there were apple turnovers of unbelievable flavor and flakiness. They ate happily till they could eat no more. Even the big German gave evidence of enjoying his supper.

There were plenty of rangers to stand guard that night, and Dick and his father turned in early. The boy slept peacefully for a solid ten hours. When he woke there was a patter of rain on the lean-to roof, and smoke from the campfire was drifting low along the ground.

"Glad this weather held off till now," Alec Campbell remarked at breakfast. "Generally we like to see plenty of rain up here in the summer, because it keeps forest fires down. But it would sure have slowed us up, getting back from Four Lakes Basin, if we'd had to travel in a storm."

As soon as breakfast was eaten they picked up their packs and started down the canyon. The footing was slippery from the rain and it was necessary to pick their way carefully. When it came to crossing the longest of the log bridges, Campbell untied the prisoner's hands so that he could keep his balance. It was a fortunate decision, for one of the big man's moccasins slipped when he was halfway across. Only the grip of his powerful arms on the bark of the log saved him from a hundred-foot fall.

They slogged along, wet and weary, all through the day. It was a mighty relief to see the glow of a lighted window in the rain and the gathering darkness, as night began to fall.

"Here you are," the Chief Ranger told the Randolphs. "Back where you started from. Better get into some dry clothes while I find out if Fong Yee's ready for visitors."

The old Chinese appeared in the doorway at that moment. He was smiling from ear to ear and shaking hands with himself in an oriental greeting.

"Velly bad night," he said in a high-pitched singsong. "You come in get supper plenty quick!"

To Alec Campbell he added the news that a Navy officer had called up from Bremerton and was now on his way over by car. Joe Evans had gone back to Seattle that afternoon.

Before Dick finished changing his clothes he heard the throb of a laboring motor coming up the last rise. The boy entered the big main room of the cabin and found quite a party gathered in front of the log fire. All four rangers were there, and with them two men in Navy uniform. He was introduced to Commander Paxton and Lieutenant Lee, both of Naval Intelligence.

"Happy to have you aboard, Randolph," the Commander told him with a smile. "I've been hearing some of the story about your part in this. I'd say you'd done quite a job, take it all in all."

"Thanks, sir," said Dick, embarrassed. "I only hope he turns out to be the man you want. Have you identified him yet?"

The officer glanced at the hulking, half-human brute, securely tied to a chair in a corner of the room. "From what Mr. Campbell tells me, I'm fairly positive," he replied. "Those duralumin pieces and the Navy 'chute-pack pretty well clinch it. But we've got photos of Dortner, and Mr. Lee, here, has seen him. After supper we'll find out for certain."

Fong Yee soon had another bountiful meal on the table. When they had finished and the Chinese was clearing away the dishes, Commander Paxton had the prisoner's chair moved under a bright light in the middle of the room.

"All right, let's get at it," said he. "Mr. Campbell, I'd like a pair of scissors and a razor if you've got them handy."

The Chief Ranger brought the items requested, along with soap, hot water and a shaving brush.

Lieutenant Lee took the scissors and started cutting away the tangled thatch of hair that hung to the cave-man's shoulders. There was murder in the giant's little red eyes, but he was powerless to do anything about it.

The young officer proceeded ruthlessly. He slashed away lock after lock of dirty hair and exposed a thick bull neck, dark with grime. Above the beetling eyebrows a round skull began to take shape.

"Well!" said Slim Harvey. "He looks less like the missin' link all the time, an' more like Von Tirpitz."

At length the hair on the man's head was cropped close to the scalp. It stood up, blond and stiff, a crude facsimile of a Prussian military haircut.

Lee's next task was to chop away the great, bristling, red beard. As it came off, the giant's whole appearance changed. A tight-lipped, sullen mouth came into view, and a jutting chin, flanked by heavy jowls. The Lieutenant stirred up some lather and applied it to the stubble, then went to work with the razor.

Commander Paxton stood close, his eyes narrowing as he watched the face that emerged. In his hand was a photograph at which he glanced from time to time. When the younger officer finished and wiped away the lather, the Commander nodded.

"It's a close enough resemblance," he said. "I suppose three years or so of the kind of animal life he's led would be bound to change a man. There's one way we can prove it beyond a doubt, though. Pull those skins off his chest,

Mr. Lee."

The Lieutenant jerked away the tattered elkhide garment and exposed a huge, muscular torso, covered with a thick mat of hair.

"Hm," grunted the Commander, stroking his chin. "He must have grown himself a fur rug, up there in the snow. We'll have to shave it off, I'm afraid."

The prisoner ground his teeth in rage as Lee wielded the brush and the razor. Commander Paxton referred to some notes on the back of the photograph he held, then leaned forward, studying the white expanse of skin laid bare by the razor.

"Now we're getting somewhere," he said grimly. "Heart and anchor tattooed on right breast. Name 'Gretchen' in German script below. That checks. Keep going, Mr. Lee. Next we should find a swastika on the left breast."

The Lieutenant applied more lather and drew the blade downward with quick, sure strokes. There on the naked flesh, sharp and ugly, was the outline of the Nazi emblem—the four bent legs of the swastika.

Lee stood back and nodded. "I'm satisfied, sir," he told the Commander. "I'd have recognized him any way, with the beard gone, but the tattoo marks make it iron-clad. We'll take fingerprints when we get back to the base, but I'd say that's just a formality after this."

Commander Paxton looked the prisoner in the eye. "You heard that, Dortner?" he asked crisply. "What have you to say?"

"Okay," said the big man, his voice low and hoarse. "I talk now."

All the resistance was gone out of his face, and his heavy chin hung slack on his chest.

"I am Anton Dortner," he continued haltingly. "Gunner on *Unterseebote sieben-acht-zwei*. Prisoner of war, escaped and recaptured. Dey put me in airplane mit armed guard und we fly nort'. Iss winter. Cold und fog. Soon makes ice on der wings. Der pilot say mus' come down a liddle. Den he see der mountain. *Bam!* We hit und fall down in deep snow. I get oudt, but odders all hurt. Den—*whoosh!* Whole t'ing burn."

He hesitated, fumbling for words. "I climb up," he went on, "und find cave. Not'ing to eat so I make bow and arrows. Five—six days, not'ing to eat. Den I kill goat. Make skis und go down der mountain. Find odder animals und kill. Come der summer I catch fish und take up der mountain. Put in lake. I got meat, fish, skin to keep warm—all iss fine. Nobody come up dere in der valley. Only I get—what iss der word—lonesome. When I catch dis boy I t'ink I keep him liddle while so I got *Kamerad*. Dere I make der big mistake. If I kill him right off, all iss fine still."

His last statement sounded so reasonable that Dick almost agreed with him. Then the full import of the man's words struck him and he shuddered in spite of himself.

The telephone on the Chief Ranger's desk rang, breaking the silence that had followed the German's recital. Campbell went over to answer it.

"Wait a minute," he said, and covered the mouthpiece with his hand. "It's the Seattle *Chronicle*," he announced with a frown. "Don't know how they got hold of the story but they want to send a man up here. What do you say, Commander?"

Paxton shrugged his shoulders and chuckled. "It's no secret any longer," he replied. "We've got all we want now. Let 'em come if they want. Better tell 'em we're leaving after breakfast in the morning, though. They can save a lot of driving by coming to Bremerton, tomorrow."

"Too late," the Chief Ranger said. "Car's on the way already." He took his palm off the transmitter.

"Okay," he told the party at the other end of the wire. "If he gets here before ten, there'll be somebody up to let him in."

Nineteen

IT WAS NINE-THIRTY WHEN THEY HEARD
a grinding of gears and spurting of gravel outside. Someone jumped out of a car and came pounding at the door
of the cabin. Craig and Harvey had already taken the
prisoner out to a shack at the rear of the Ranger Station,
where they would guard him through the night. It was
Alec Campbell who went to the door.

The young man who entered was shaking water off his

raincoat.

"Jensen, of the *Chronicle*," he announced briskly. "I've got a cameraman along, and he'll be here in a minute. What's the story? Where's this prehistoric man I heard about?"

The Chief Ranger puffed at his pipe and looked the reporter over. Then he nodded courteously.

"Come in, Mr. Jensen," said he. "Meet my guests. Commander Paxton and Lieutenant Lee, of the Navy, and Dr. Randolph and Dick Randolph."

Jensen curbed his impatience with a visible effort. He shook hands around the circle, then went to the door himself to admit his partner, a stout individual by the name of McGill. The photographer was carrying a big Graflex camera and a folded tripod. He, too, was introduced, and when both men had been given chairs by the fire, the Chief Ranger nodded toward Paxton. There was a twinkle in his eye.

"The Navy's in charge now," he said. "Any questions you want to ask should be addressed to the Commander."

The reporter was unabashed. "Well," he said, "we understand there's a big story here and we'd like to break it ahead of the competition. Is it true you've captured some kind of a Stone Age character?"

"That certainly is what he looks like," Commander Paxton smiled. "That is—he did until a couple of hours ago. Now he's just an oversized German sailor. His hair and beard, if you'd be interested, are in the wastebasket over there."

The cameraman looked sick. "You mean you clipped 'em off?" he exclaimed. "An' didn't wait for a picture?"

The Navy officer nodded. "Sorry," said he, "but we had to do it to make sure who he was. Maybe you recall when one of our planes was reported missing with a German war prisoner aboard? It was back in February of 'forty-four, but no announcement was made until months later."

He went on to give a brief outline of the story while Jensen scribbled furiously in his notebook.

"Tonight," Commander Paxton concluded, "we made the identification complete. Dortner has been living up there in the high peaks for over three years. Do you wonder that he looked like a caveman?"

The news photographer clutched his hair and groaned. "But no pictures!" he repeated sorrowfully. "Well, I guess the best we can do is a shot o' the guy like he is now. Is he around somewhere?"

"He's asleep," the Commander replied firmly. "Asleep and under guard. I'm afraid you'll have to wait till morning. I do have an extra print of this photo, though. It's a good likeness, taken before the plane crash."

He held out the small photograph and Jensen took it eagerly. "Good!" he said. "Tough-looking hombre, all right. Say, Chief, mind if I use your phone? I'd like to get this piece in the early edition. Then we'll rush the picture back to town, an' make the city edition with a big spread on page one."

Dick had been trying to say something, but the reporter was too full of business to listen. He talked fast into the telephone, shooting the main facts to a rewrite man.

"I'll be there in two hours," he finished. "Got a picture with me, but you might have 'em dig one up in the morgue too, if they've got it. Yeah—Anton Dortner's the name. I'm starting right now."

He clapped on his hat and seized McGill by the arm. "Come on," he barked. "We've got to drive fast. Thanks, Commander."

With that he was out of the door, with the photographer lugging his equipment sadly after him. Dick heard the whirr of the starter. Then, before the car was moving, there came the sound of other vehicles churning up the trail.

Outside in the rain a voice shouted, "Who's there? That you, Jensen?"

"Yep!" the reporter answered with a laugh. "Too bad, old man! Beat you to it this time."

He trod on the accelerator, turned his car and went bumping away down the hill.

"Gee!" Dick murmured. "If he hadn't been in such a rush I'd have told him about that film in my camera. I got some swell shots of Dortner up there on the mountain."

Commander Paxton tipped back his head and roared with laughter. "Serves the young squirt right!" he said. "But we seem to have some more callers. I wonder who's barging in this time of night."

They weren't left long in doubt. Two men came hurrying to the half-open door and almost collided in their eagerness to be first into the room.

The Chief Ranger bristled. "Take it easy, gentlemen," he said grimly. "Perhaps you'll tell me your errand?"

Both men started speaking at once, but the gray-haired, heavy-set one talked louder and got the first hearing.

"I'm K. D. Gordon, Consolidated News Syndicate," he explained with a bow. "Glad to see you again, Chief. Hear you've got a news story."

Campbell nodded noncommittally. "And you, sir?" he asked the other newcomer—a squirrel-faced little man who carried a heavy camera case.

"Zenith Photo Service," came the answer. "Havens is the name—Jimmy Havens. Happy to meet you, sir."

His disarming grin won a less formal greeting from the Chief Ranger. "Well, well," he said, thawing, "the Press is out in force tonight. Pull up to the fire, gentlemen."

Again the introductions were made, and again Commander Paxton summarized the facts in the case. When he finished, Gordon leaned forward, tapping his pencil against his teeth.

"That," he remarked musingly, "is quite a yarn. Handled right, it's front page, clear across the country. My angle on it is that it's the boy's story—your story, Dick. I'm not even sure we couldn't make a three-or-four-part feature out of it. Jensen's scooped us with the bare facts but I'll bet he didn't see what was in it. Did he ask you any questions, Dick?"

The boy shook his head. "No," he said. "He just phoned in what the Commander told him."

"Well," Gordon smiled, "I know it's late so I won't bother you tonight. I'll just call our Seattle office and give them a flash to put on the wire. Then, if you could find a cot for me to sleep on, Chief, I'd like to tackle the real job in the morning."

The man from Zenith Photo Service had been looking around the room, his bright eyes darting here and there. Now he spoke abruptly to Dick.

"Like to take pictures?" he asked.

"Sure. How did you know?"

"I saw your camera case over there by your pack. From the way it's scratched up, I guess you took it with you on this trip. Get any good shots of the caveman while he still looked the part?"

"He did," Commander Paxton interrupted, and there was a smile twitching at the corners of his mouth. "I think you'd be open to a real business offer, wouldn't you, Dick?"

"Yes, sir," said Dick, trying not to look too excited. "I took pictures of Dortner with his beard and skin clothes and everything. There's one close-up that ought to be really good. Then I got some shots of the cave and the peaks—eight or ten in all."

Havens' eyes were brighter than ever. "Let me have that film," he said, "and we'll pay you fifty dollars apiece for each negative that's good enough to use."

"Three hundred for the lot, sight unseen," snapped Gordon. "And another five hundred for the story."

"Any further bidding, gentlemen?" the Commander asked politely.

The two men glared at each other for a moment, then both saw the humorous side of the affair.

"I'll make a dicker with you, K.D.," Havens smiled. "I'll give Consolidated exclusive rights on three of the pictures—any three you want—at a hundred apiece. And I'll throw in a couple of shots of Dick, so you can use 'em in your serial feature. I figure we can do all right with what's left, because I'm gambling on this lad's being a pretty smart cameraman. Suppose there are eight good negatives in the lot. That gives Dick four hundred dollars, plus the five hundred you pay him for the story. What do you say, folks? Is that a fair deal all around?"

Dr. Randolph glanced at Dick, then at the Commander. "It sounds generous enough to me," he answered, "if Mr. Gordon's satisfied."

Gordon nodded. "Okay with me," he said. "Here, I'll

put it in memorandum form and we'll all sign it."

Dick's head was in a whirl as he looked at the figures on the paper. He wrote his name under that of his father and passed the sheet along to Havens. When all the signatures were on it, Alec Campbell took the memorandum and put it in the office strongbox.

"Now," said the Chief, trying to hide a yawn, "I think we're all ready for bed."

.   .   .

The Ranger Station was a beehive of activity the next morning. The rain was over and a bright sun shone on the glittering forest. Havens had his camera set up before breakfast, and by eight o'clock he had taken pictures of Dortner, of the three blackened skulls, and of all the other articles found in the cave. Shortly after that the two Navy officers set off for Bremerton with their prisoner, taking Slim Harvey along to act as an extra guard.

Commander Paxton shook Dick's hand before he got into the car. "I'm glad you're going to be paid for this job, son," he said. "And you've earned every cent of it. If Campbell doesn't get you for the Forest Service we'd like to have you in the Navy."

The boy reddened with pleasure. "I'll think about it, sir," he answered. "I want to go to college, and if my exams are good enough, maybe I can do it as a Navy trainee."

"Fine!" said the Commander. "Good luck, and if there's anything I can do to help, let me know."

Dick found K. D. Gordon waiting for him when he came back to the cabin.

"I was planning to go over your story here," said the veteran newspaperman. "But I believe I've got a better idea. If you and your father are ready to start back, I'll take you to Seattle in my car. Then we can go right to the Consolidated office and I'll have a stenographer take down the whole tale in your own words. It'll be quicker, and we'll have a chance to look over the pictures as soon as Havens develops 'em."

"Sounds fine," said Dick. "Let me check with Dad."

Dr. Randolph agreed to the plan, and as soon as they could assemble their belongings they were ready to leave. Jimmy Havens held up the departure for a few minutes while he took some camera shots of Dick in his trail-worn mountain clothes, carrying his pack. Then the boy and his father said good-bye to their ranger friends and the two cars started down the rough road beside the Dosewallips.

Reaching the highway they swung south along the shore of the Hood Canal. The road led through little towns with such picturesque names as Lilliwaup, Hoodsport and Potlatch, then doubled back around the fishhook bend of the canal and headed northeast toward Bremerton. There they made the eleven o'clock ferry and were in Seattle by lunch time.

Havens had Dick's black-and-white film when he left them at the ferry house. "I'll go right to work on these," he said. "Ought to have the prints in two or three hours. I'll give you a call at Consolidated."

Gordon drove the Randolphs to the hotel and stood by while they got a room, bathed and changed into more presentable clothes. Then they ate a hasty lunch and Dick went with the newspaperman to the big downtown office building where Consolidated had its local headquarters. Dr. Randolph stayed behind to make a plane reservation and do some telephoning.

They entered a large room, noisy with the click of teletype machines. Gordon led the way back to a smaller and quieter office at the rear. In a few minutes Dick found himself seated at a table, trying to gather his thoughts. Across from him was a capable-looking girl with pencil poised above her shorthand notebook.

"Just relax," Gordon told him gently. "Tell it the way you'd tell some of the gang back at school. You don't need to worry about grammar or anything. I'll fix that up."

The boy looked out the window at the blue of Puget Sound and the snowy peaks of the Olympics beyond.

"Well," he began, "it all started with my wanting to see some real wilderness—that, and the Smithsonian needing silver marmots for a habitat group. When I got off the plane at Seattle, I never thought that inside of two weeks I'd be mixed up with anything as weird as a cave-man killer right out of the Stone Age."

"Swell!" murmured Gordon. "That's the stuff. Keep going, boy."

And keep going he did for the better part of two hours. Occasionally the reporter prompted him with a question, but when he got into the swing of his narrative it flowed more easily than he had expected. He described the hidden valley, the climb to the chimney, the discovery of the cached elk meat, and finally his capture by the huge, red-bearded man in skins. The terror of those hours in the cave was so vivid in his memory that he made it come alive in words. When he brought the story to its end he felt almost as tired as if he had climbed and struggled and starved all over again.

Gordon stood up and clapped him on the shoulder. He looked excited. "Great!" he said. "We'll spread that from coast to coast. You're going to be famous, son!"

"Gosh," said Dick, in awe, "it didn't sound so hot to me. I sure hope you'll polish it up before it gets in the papers. My English teacher never thought I was very good at compositions."

The telephone rang and Gordon answered it. "Good!" he said. "Yes, we're both ready. Bring 'em along."

He replaced the receiver. "That's Havens," he reported. "He's on his way over with the pictures."

The photographer burst into the room a few minutes later like a small whirlwind.

"Look!" he cried. "Ten of 'em—all beauties! Didn't I tell you this boy could handle a camera? Here's your check from Zenith, Dick, and it reads five hundred dollars!"

On the table he spread the prints. With blurred eyes Dick looked into the snarling face of the caveman—saw the big, shaggy brute wrestling with his captors. There were clear-cut pictures of the cave mouth, of Campbell holding the loot found there, and of the majestic sea of mountains viewed from the ledge. Finally there were photographs of Dortner, shaved and with his hair cropped, and others of Dick, equipped for the trail. He felt a thrill as he stared at his own likeness, realizing it would soon be on hundreds of newspaper pages.

"What do you say, K.D.?" asked Havens. "Like 'em?"

"You're right about their all being good, Jimmy," the reporter grinned. "In fact I'm having a tough time picking my three."

Again the telephone rang. This time it was Dr. Randolph, asking for Dick.

"There's an eastbound plane leaving at eight tonight," he said. "If Gordon's finished with you, I've got a couple of seats through to Washington. Think you can be ready?"

"Sure," the boy replied. "I'll be back at the hotel to pack in half an hour."

He shook hands with Gordon and Havens and left the

building, walking on air. In his pocket were two checks that totaled a thousand dollars!

.   .   .

Dick and his father dined leisurely on Seattle's most famous dish, cracked Dungeness crab, and took the limousine to the airport. The two marmot skins had been entrusted to an expert taxidermist for treatment before shipping to Washington. Dr. Randolph had his specimens with him in his luggage.

It was a fine, clear evening, and as they walked out on the airstrip, the botanist pointed to the southeast, where Mt. Rainier towered in grandeur against the turquoise sky.

"Well, son," he said, "what do you think of this Puget Sound country, now you've seen it?"

Dick's eyes glowed. "It's been pretty good to me," he grinned. "I don't think I'll be really happy till I get out here again—maybe for keeps."

"Hm," said his father, with a nod of understanding. "I know what you mean. It's a young man's country. And you still like the Olympics?"

"The Olympics best of all," said Dick, and meant it.

THE END